Praise for
KATHRYN WINTER'S
Katarina

★ "First-rate fiction, it marks the author as someone to watch."
—*Publishers Weekly*, starred review

"First-time novelist Kathryn Winter, drawing on her own childhood experiences, creates an intimate portrait of a girl caught up in events beyond her understanding....[Winter] offers richly detailed memories and asks the reader to serve as witness to the events these memories recount."

—*The New York Times Book Review*

"This book bears testament to the pernicious influences of insularity and superstition and to the courage of people who, in the face of danger, are willing to defend the helpless....*Katarina* is worth reading and begs for discussion. Winter has told her story with admirable evenness....Teachers, librarians, and parents should find ample use for this powerful book."

—*School Library Journal*

"There is a dramatic immediacy in the child's bewildered view of the shifting realities she must get used to in order to survive.... [Winter's] story will move readers with its honesty about her survival and the horror she escaped."

—*Booklist*

Other Signature Titles

Bad Girls
Cynthia Voigt

Bad, Badder, Baddest
Cynthia Voigt

Clockwork
Philip Pullman

Faith and the Electric Dogs
Patrick Jennings

The Fire Pony
Rodman Philbrick

Jonah, the Whale
Susan Shreve

The Library Card
Jerry Spinelli

The Music of Dolphins
Karen Hesse

Out of the Dust
Karen Hesse

Perloo
Avi

P.S. Longer Letter Later
Ann M. Martin and
Paula Danziger

Riding Freedom
Pam Muñoz Ryan

Somewhere in the Darkness
Walter Dean Myers

*Stay True: Short Stories for
Strong Girls*
edited by Marilyn Singer

Tangerine
Edward Bloor

Trout Summer
Jane Lesley Conly

Tru Confessions
Janet Tashjian

The Van Gogh Cafe
Cynthia Rylant

Katarína

a novel by Kathryn Winter

SCHOLASTIC
Signature

an imprint of
Scholastic Inc.

New York • Toronto • London • Auckland • Sydney
Mexico City • New Delhi • Hong Kong

FOR LENA

ACKNOWLEDGMENTS

For information on the persecution of Jews in Slovakia I consulted the historian Ivan Kamenec and his book *In the Footsteps of Tragedy*.

I thank my friends and fellow writers in Thursday's Child for encouraging me to write this book. My special thanks to Lee Prickett Wagner, Kathryn Vergeer, Horacio Miller, Margaret DuBois, Margo Feeley, Marilyn and Nelson Goodman, Mark Greenside, and my editor at Farrar, Straus and Giroux, Robbie Mayes.

CONTENTS

Slovakia: Historical Note   *xi*

A Brief Pronunciation Guide to Slovak Names   *xiii*

Prologue   *3*

Snowdrops   *5*

Dear Eva   *24*

Saints   *35*

The Secret   *41*

The Husárs' Barn   *49*

Spring Rites   *63*

One Dried Spider, Three Cat Whiskers   *77*

Parting   *92*

Katarína Waits   *101*

Town Crier   *121*

Headquarters   *128*

Stefie   *132*

Seven Voices   *146*

God's Plan   *162*

Krmanov's Home of Love   *179*

The War   *194*

Liberated   *210*

Orava, My River   *230*

Remembering   *249*

Epilogue   *257*

SLOVAKIA: HISTORICAL NOTE

World War I broke up the Austro-Hungarian Empire. A number of small countries were created in its place, among them Czechoslovakia. It was believed that allowing ethnic minorities to have their own countries would prevent future world wars.

For more than twenty years Czechoslovakia prospered as a free, democratic country in the heart of Europe. Then, on March 15, 1939, German forces occupied Bohemia and Moravia, the Czech sections of the country. Slovakia declared its independence and became a puppet state controlled by Germany. It provided rail and road access to the East for the Germans, and after the German attack on the Soviet Union, fighting troops as well. In return, Slovakia enjoyed significant benefits such as increased trade and help in industrial development. Slovakia's state police, the Hlinka Guard, most willingly helped carry out Hitler's plan to exterminate the Jews of Europe.

A Brief Pronunciation Guide to Slovak Names

Generally, in pronouncing Slovak words, the stress is on the first syllable. When a vowel has an accent over it, like the "í" in Katarína, the sound is prolonged. Most consonants are pronounced as in English, with a few exceptions noted below, and "r"s are rolled. When the ˇ symbol (called a háček) is placed atop a consonant, its sound is softened.

a	ah (hard)
c	ts (pizza)
č	ch (chalk)
ch	kh (pronounced as a lengthened, throaty "k" sound)
e	eh (bed)
g	g (always hard, as in goose)
i	ih (chin)
j	y (yes)
ň	ny (Kenya)
o	oh (north)
š	sh (shout)
u	oo (foot)
y	ih (chin)
ž	zh (pleasure)

KATARÍNA

PROLOGUE

J anuary 1942. The fields surrounding T——, a small village in northern Slovakia, lie deep under snow.

The passenger train slows as it rounds the curve along the frozen pond. Children on skates rush to the pond's edge to wave.

One child, alone, stands with her back to the train, facing the empty fields.

SNOWDROPS

Katarína, come to the window, look!"

That's Eva. I know what she wants to show me. Snowdrops. She must have rushed to the fields with Kristína at the first sound of the river cracking. Last year I froze my fingers digging for them in the snow, but Eva had the luck. "Hey, I found one, I found the first snowdrop!" and she held it up for all of us to see: drooping white petals on a stem thin as thread.

"Hey, Katarína, come look!"

Stupid Eva. Shout all you want, I'm not coming to the window. I pull the covers over my head. Stupid snowdrops!

There is a red sign tacked to our front door: KEEP OUT! SCARLET FEVER. FEBRUARY 26, 1942. THE BOARD OF HEALTH. The sign has been there over a month.

I don't have scarlet fever. Only make-believe. I'd woken up the night Aunt Lena was rubbing me with ointment.

5

"What are you doing?"

"Something I need to do, Katinka. Try to sleep."

"Hey, stop. It stinks."

I slipped out of bed and ducked behind the armchair.

"Come back. I need to rub on some more."

"Why?"

Silence.

"If you tell me why, I'll let you."

They were rounding up Jews, she said, to send to work camps. The ointment was to make my skin break out in red blotches, and in the morning she'd give me a red candy to coat my tongue and throat. If we were lucky, it would fool the doctor—he'd think I had scarlet fever and he'd give us a sign to post on our door that read KEEP OUT! "That means the Hlinka Guards, too, Katinka. It can save us."

Save us? I peered at my aunt from behind the armchair. From what, work? Why shouldn't we help if our country needed us? I'll ask her that, but not now. Now was my chance to find out something else.

"Who is he?"

"What do you mean?"

"That *someone* you see each time you pack me off to Malka's house."

She blushed. I was on the right track.

"What's his name?"

"Teodor. Uncle Teo to you."

"*Uncle* Teo. You're going to marry him?"

Her lips tightened, but she wasn't angry—I can tell when she is. There was mischief in her eyes.

"Are you?"

"Yes. Now come back here, you little—"

"Yes? Did you say yes? A real wedding, with music and dancing? When?"

"As soon as this madness blows over and things settle back to normal. Katinka, I need to rub on more of that ointment."

"If I let you—no school?"

"No school."

"For how long?"

"I don't know. Stop being difficult. Please!"

I got out from behind the chair. Stretched. Aunt Lena looked like a little bird on a windowsill trying to get inside, where it's warm. At this moment I could have made her promise me anything. A later bedtime. A sheepskin vest like the one Eva wears. Let my hair grow long enough to braid. Dumplings once a week and never again spinach or squash. But, the next thing, I was running across the room, flinging my arms around her neck.

"Don't be sad, Lena-bird, I won't be difficult." I pulled her to my bed. "Rub on that stinky ointment."

At first quarantine was fun. Aunt Lena read to me, told me stories about herself and my mother when they were children, made dumplings and chocolate pudding whenever I asked her to. We played dominoes, exercised on the floor, danced to tunes we hummed, made up skits we acted out. I liked acting out what happened the day we fooled the doctor.

"You be the doctor, Aunt Lena."

She'd squint, puff on a make-believe pipe, shake her head.

"What's wrong, Doctor?"

A sigh from her.

"Nothing serious, is it?"

"My dear lady . . . those red patches on her skin . . . the red tongue and throat . . ."

"Yes?"

A long pause. Then: "I am afraid the child has scarlet fever."

At this I'd faint, but after a few seconds my eyes would flutter open.

"How awful, Doctor. Are you certain?"

"The symptoms are unmistakable."

"What do we do?"

"We'll have her admitted to the isolation unit at the county hospital. They already have one case of scarlet fever."

"No! I won't allow it. I'll not have Katarína exposed to—"

"Exposed? But, dear lady, she has already succumbed."

"Yes, of course . . . I meant I'll not have her confined in that overcrowded hospital, I'll nurse her myself, here at home."

"I'd have to put you under quarantine—"

"Yes, of course."

"—with no one allowed to enter or leave this house for six weeks. How will you manage?"

"We have enough provisions stored in the pantry. Our helper, Janko Trnka, can bring other things we need from his farm and leave them on the porch."

"I'll get a KEEP OUT sign, to post on your door . . ."

"Yes, Doctor."

"Six weeks. Is that clear?"

Clear and wonderful. No school for six weeks. I watched Aunt Lena walk the doctor out of the room, listened to the bells of his sleigh as he rode off, then leaped out of bed.

"Hooray, we did it!"

Her hand covered my mouth. "Quiet. They can hear us outside."

They could hear but couldn't see in through the frost-covered window. Aunt Lena hugged me, lifted me, swung me around. We danced a polka around the room until we collapsed on my bed, dizzy and giggling.

That first week I gloated, hearing Eva and her friend Kristína pass by my window in the early morning. They were going to school while I snuggled under my eiderdown. But the second week I wished I were going with them. The third week I cried, "Aunt Lena, how much longer?"

I can't go to school but I have to do homework just the same. For two hours a day Aunt Lena gives me lessons, then checks my work with a red pencil, like a teacher. It's lucky the violin is out of the house or she'd make me practice, like she used to—nag, nag, every day. But just a short time before our quarantine, on my way home from school, I saw a crowd in front of the post office. The town crier was reading his announcements.

"Item. Jews are to turn in all coats and jackets made of fur or leather.

"Item. Jews are to turn in valuables made of gold, silver, ivory, or bronze.

"Item. Jews are to give up musical instruments. Jewish families in possession of a piano, violin, flute, accordion, harmonica . . ."

I didn't stay to listen for more. I raced home with the news.

"The swine," Aunt Lena mumbled. "They don't know where to stop."

On the day the instruments were to be taken, I waited for the policemen at the window, then followed the one carrying my violin out the door.

"Don't change your mind," I begged.

"What?"

"Don't bring that violin back. Promise?"

Two weeks later I ran after him, howling. He was taking away my sled!

I wasn't at home when they took the radio and the Victrola. I found out after supper, the time we usually listened to music. That evening Aunt Lena and I sat in the kitchen hiding our tears behind the steaming cups of milk with honey we were sipping. I didn't know I was tapping a rhythm on my cup until she answered me, on hers: *tap, tap, tip-tip, tap.* We looked up at the same time and burst out laughing. Her taps sounded higher than mine. She said it was because her cup was thinner and nearly empty. I tapped the milk pitcher, the honey jar, the sugar bowl. Soon all the cups, glasses, pots, and bowls were off the shelves and on the kitchen table. *Tap, tap,* with my knuckles, a fork, a wooden spoon. On the outside, the bottom, the rim. "Let's pour water into this bowl." *Tap.* "Now pour some out." "Where is the washboard?" "Here, try the eggbeater." "Can you reach the mortar and pestle?" *Tap, rub, scratch.* "Aunt Lena, this old blue basin makes more sounds than an orchestra."

We stayed up long past my bedtime finding sounds we liked, composing short pieces. Every object in the house had turned into a musical instrument.

I am bored doing nothing, but there is nothing I want to do. Will I ever catch up with schoolwork? It's lucky the principal likes Aunt Lena and lets me go to the village school. But will Aunt Lena let me go back when the KEEP OUT! sign comes down, or will she teach me herself, at home, as she told the Rabbi she would? At least I definitely won't have to go to the one-room school again. I hated it. It had been the Rabbi's idea. "Send her to us," he told Aunt Lena back in November, "where she belongs. Let her learn what it means to be a Jew. I've made room in my house. We have an excellent teacher. The five Jewish families are sharing the cost . . ."

Twelve students, one teacher, all the grades together in one room. Malka and I in third grade. The teacher working with one grade at a time, keeping the others busy

copying pages from textbooks, memorizing multiplication tables, spelling lists, poems. I told Aunt Lena it was
boring, that I wanted to be with Eva. I didn't tell her
that the Jewish children whispered secrets to one another and called me *the heathen*.

For that, too, the Rabbi is to blame. On my first day he
walked in with books piled up to his chin. Bibles. The
class read out loud, in Hebrew. I mumbled along, pretending to follow the text, but forgot to move my head
from right to left instead of from left to right. The Rabbi
noticed.

"Stand up, Katarína. Read us the passage we just read."

My cheeks were burning. I had never learned the Hebrew alphabet.

"So!" The Rabbi stood there, nodding, stroking his
beard. "Tell us, Katarína, what Jewish holiday is coming
up, and how do we celebrate it?"

"Christmas?" I mumbled. I knew it was the wrong answer, but I couldn't remember the name of the holiday
Malka's family celebrated.

The room heaved with laughter. Even my friend, sour-
puss Malka, was shrieking. But the Rabbi did not laugh.

"So. We have a heathen among us. A little heathen."

I had to beg Aunt Lena for two weeks before she let
me go back to the village school. Three days later the
Rabbi came knocking on our door.

"What are you doing, Lena? The girl isn't learning a
thing about being Jewish except to be ashamed of it.
Your goy helper, Janko Trnka, knows more about our hol-

idays, our way of life, than she does. Do you think your sister, may she rest in peace—"

"Yes, do let her rest in peace. I am the one raising Katarína."

"Then raise her to become a good Jewish woman."

Aunt Lena's voice dropped, I couldn't hear her. I heard the Rabbi.

"A what, a good person? How very broad-minded. Come to your senses, Lena. Bad things are happening to us and they'll get worse—"

"They won't. Our President is a Catholic priest, he'll let things go only so far—"

"You amaze me, Lena. Have you heard of the Inquisition?"

"That was in the Middle Ages. We're in the twentieth century. The civilized world won't allow—"

"Civilized world! You should have seen my nine-year-old, how he'd come home from the village school. A bloody nose. Torn clothes. A black eye. His classmates would beat him up while the *civilized* teachers watched. That's why I started our own school, even before the law was passed. And that's another reason you should send Katarína to us. If anyone reports to Headquarters that she, a Jewish child, is attending public school, the entire Jewish community of this village will be penalized. You're putting us all at risk."

For a while it was quiet in the room. Then Aunt Lena said, "All right. I'll see, maybe I'll teach her myself, at home. Katarína did not adjust to the one-room school, and you know how I feel about religion. It divides people, creates suffering—"

"Yes, Lena. 'All mankind shall be brothers.' A pity the Germans don't listen to their poet Schiller and the Slovaks don't give a damn about your liberal ideas. It makes no difference what you think or do. You are a Jew, so is she, and no one will let you forget it."

The Rabbi was right, they wouldn't let me forget in the village school that I am a Jew; in the Jewish school, that I am a heathen. They called me a heathen because I know nothing about religion, "Redhead" because of my red hair, "Freckleface" because of my freckles. But what makes me Jewish? When the Rabbi left that day, I asked Aunt Lena.

"In our religion, if the mother is Jewish, so is the child," she told me.

"But my mother wasn't religious, was she? And we aren't, either."

"It's not just a religion, Katinka. The Jews have a common history, common values, traditions. A way of life."

"Like what?"

"Like lighting candles on Friday night or during Hanukkah—"

Hanukkah! That's what I should have answered when the Rabbi asked me about the coming Jewish holiday. "What does Hanukkah mean?"

"More than two thousand years ago, when the Jews lived in their own country, they rebelled against the Syrian King Antiochus. Jews light candles to celebrate—"

"But *we* don't light candles. Only on birthday cakes. Why are *we* Jewish?"

"I don't have an answer, Katinka, and those who do, keep changing it. Once they defined 'Jewish' as a religion, then as a race, then an anti-race—"

"A what? I don't understand."

"No one does. It makes no sense. You and I eat bacon and don't observe any religious holidays, but no matter what we think or do, we're still Jewish."

Aunt Lena sounded like the Rabbi. A way of life, she said. Malka is Jewish, and her "way of life" isn't anything like mine. Eva is Catholic, and hers is. With Malka, it's always "I'm supposed to" or "I'm not supposed to." Supposed to pray, fast, wear long sleeves and stockings even in the summer. Not supposed to eat this food or use those dishes. "I can't eat dairy food with meat," she said once, when I offered her crackers with salami and cheese. "Is there any jam?" At home or at Eva's house we eat bread and butter with a thick slice of ham on whatever dishes. Or no dishes. Eva and I would sometimes roast bacon on spits over an open fire and eat it with our fingers when it was cool enough to touch. After school she, Kristína, and I would ride on our sleds until it got too dark to see. And when my sled was taken away they let me ride on theirs. Malka never came with us. She is not supposed to play with the village children. Not supposed to climb trees, wade in the brook, roast potatoes in the field. Fridays, with no homework to worry about, Eva and I would play together till suppertime. Malka would run home from her one-room school to get ready for the Sabbath.

Malka's way of life isn't like mine at all.

Spring is on its way—I can hear it. Snow sliding off our roof, icicles dripping, boots slushing through puddles. The ice on Eva's pond must be getting too soft for skating.

When their pond froze in November, Eva invited Kristína, me, and other classmates to skate. I went every afternoon.

One day, soon after Christmas, Eva told me I couldn't come anymore. "Why?" I asked. "What's wrong, are you mad at me?" Eva shrugged, shook her head. "My mother made me tell you."

"But why? What did I do?"

She burst out crying, turned around, and ran.

I told Aunt Lena. "I know, Katinka. That silly woman spoke to me." Then, in a high-pitched voice, to sound like Eva's mother, she said, " 'I'm sorry, Miss Lena. It's nothing personal, Katarína is a well-behaved little girl. But you know, my husband works for the government, we can't have a Jewish child coming to our home or skating on our property . . .' Don't be sad, Katinka," she said in her own voice. "We'll go to the Orava River. I'll help you clear a space of snow, you can skate on the ice there, I'll stay with you—"

"No," I cried. "I want to be with the other children. I am like Eva and Kristína. I am like *them*."

Eva cried and begged until her mother said, "All right,

Katarína may come skate, but she mustn't show her face." I'd bundle up so that only my eyes and the tip of my nose showed. Whenever a train passed, all the children would rush to the edge of the pond, to wave. Sometimes I'd rush along with them and then Eva would tug at my sleeve to remind me—I mustn't show my face. And I would turn to stand with my back to the train.

Thunder. Today, at noon, I heard it. It's the ice in the river cracking.

Each spring, that sound is like a whistle that starts a race—all the girls in the village rush to the fields to find the first snowdrop.

I jumped out of bed, got dressed, tiptoed down the hallway.

"Hey, where are you going?"

Aunt Lena caught me at the front door in my coat and boots. She must have heard the floorboards creaking.

"Answer me. Where are you going?"

"Out, to look for snowdrops."

"Get back to bed, at once."

"No! I want to be out there, with the other children. I won't stay locked up in here forever."

"Not forever, Katarína; for ten more days. Now get into bed, people can see in."

"Let them. Let them see I'm not sick, that you're *making* me stay in bed. Let everybody know how mean you are."

·   ·   ·

"Aunt Lena, show me that newspaper story again."

I know the story by heart. Two yellowed pages my aunt saved from five years ago. An avalanche in the Tatra Mountains that killed six skiers. There is a picture of them. My father is dark, good-looking, my mother fair, like Aunt Lena, and even prettier. They are both smiling. I bet *they* wouldn't have rubbed that stinky ointment on me to make me look sick. They'd have gone to help out in the camp and taken me with them.

"Why didn't you rub that ointment on your own skin, Aunt Lena, make yourself look sick?"

"I wish I could have, Katinka. But do you think the doctor would have let me stay at home, in care of a not yet eight-year-old nurse?"

She is right, but that doesn't make it any easier for me.

"How much longer before I can go back to school?"

"Our quarantine ends in five days, but you won't be going back to school here. We'll be moving, to live with Uncle Teo."

"We will? Is that why you've been writing each other all those letters?"

She nods.

"I don't want to leave Eva."

"It's sad, Katinka, I know. She is your best friend."

"Why can't Uncle Teo come here, live with us?"

"He is a lawyer and he needs to stay in his village."

"But Jews are not allowed to be lawyers anymore. That's why Malka's uncle had to move in with them. He isn't allowed to work, she said."

"Uncle Teo has an exemption from President Tiso because there are no other lawyers where he lives."

"And where is that? Is it close enough for Eva and me to visit often?"

"It's about two hours by bus. But, Katinka, Eva's mother might not let her visit often. She isn't happy that the two of you are so close."

"Aunt Lena, please, let's not leave."

"You'll make new friends in school—"

"Won't you be teaching me at home, like you told the Rabbi?"

"No. You will go to the public school because they have no other. The few Jews who live there are elderly couples with grown children."

"I'll be so lonely without Eva."

"Uncle Teo has a son, Pavel. I am sure the two of you will—"

"He won't count. He is a boy."

"Not a boy, Katinka. He is twenty-one."

"Twenty-one? That's grownup. He doesn't count *double*."

Two or three times a week after the last light in the village goes out, Aunt Lena bundles me up and takes me out into the yard.

"Breathe deeply, Katinka," she whispers. "You need the fresh air."

The first three weeks of quarantine, when our boots would squeak on the frozen snow, Aunt Lena was afraid the neighbors might hear. We'd creep to the darkest corner and stand there, huddling, watching the stars. Now that there are only patches of soft gray snow left and I can wear my sheepskin slippers outside, she tells me, "Run to the well and back, Katinka. You need the exercise."

How I wished, those first weeks, that I could run. To the well, past it, and out to the frozen pastures behind the barns. I often dreamed of running across wide, open meadows, of skipping over rivulets of melting snow, of sliding over long patches of ice in the frozen river.

"Go on, don't be lazy."

Now that our windows are clear of frost and people can see in, Aunt Lena has been making me stay in bed or else sit quietly by the stove. My legs feel like dough. I don't want to run. I no longer dream about running.

Our helper, Janko Trnka, chops wood for our three stoves, scrapes ice off the porch steps, and leaves bread, milk, cheese, and eggs from his farm at our door. He also brings Uncle Teo's letters from the post office and mails Aunt Lena's.

Janko is a hunched old man with a goiter so large it hangs from his neck in a dirty pouch. Today, for the first time, he is allowed inside the house. I can hear him stacking logs in the kitchen.

"Janko Trnka," I shout into the hallway, "have you seen my friend Malka?"

"She gone," he calls back in his thick, raspy voice. "The whole family gone."

Where are they, I wonder—in a work camp? They won't keep Malka long with all her "supposed to's" and "not supposed to's." "Excuse me, I have to stop working, it's time to light candles for the Sabbath." "Sorry, I can't drink milk with meat. Is there any lemonade?" Malka will come back, and so will Shaiko, her little brother. What could he do there, anyway? Peel carrots? Help set the table? He can't see over the tabletop if he stands on tiptoes!

"Aunt Lena, how come they send children to work camps?"

"They don't. Only people aged sixteen to thirty. Malka's family must be hiding to protect her two older sisters."

"Our principal at school talked to us about the camps. He said the work is good for the people who do it, good for their families, and good for our country."

"Aren't we fortunate—a triple blessing. I wonder what keeps him from sending off his three buxom daughters."

"He says that the camp workers take work over from Slovak soldiers and then the soldiers can go help the Germans fight the Russians."

"That's not true, Katinka. The young people are being deported, sent out of the country against their will. And only Jews. That's prejudice."

Prejudice always upsets Aunt Lena. She worries about Czechs, Gypsies, Protestants, about people who lose their jobs or don't get paid enough. She was once arrested, when we lived in the city, for handing out leaflets about labor unions. I have heard Eva's mother call Aunt Lena a "Jewish Bolshevik atheist with her head in the clouds."

"Do you think Malka will be back soon?"

"I don't know. They might be hiding in this village, as we've been doing. Or they might have gone to Hungary. Jews can live in peace there, and Malka's mother is part-Hungarian."

"Will they come back after the war?"

No answer.

"Aunt Lena, will they?"

"I think they will. Their home is here. Katinka, aren't you forgetting something very important? You don't remember what day it is?"

I shake my head.

"It's the last day of our quarantine. You've been waiting for this—"

"Aunt Lena, you're not thirty yet, are you?"

"Not until October. Why?"

"They can still get you to go to that work camp, can't they?"

"This roundup is over. It only lasted a few days. We stayed locked up longer, to make believe the scarlet fever was real."

"Will there be another one? Can they take you away while I'm in school?"

"No one will take me away. Uncle Teo's exemption will protect me. Katinka, didn't you hear what I said? We can go *out* tomorrow."

"Do you remember, Aunt Lena, when the doctor wanted to send me to the county hospital?"

"Oh, yes. I was frightened to death that he would."

"If he had, would they have taken you to the work camp without me?"

She shakes her head.

"You wouldn't let anyone take you anywhere without me, would you?"

"No, of course not."

"Aunt Lena—promise?"

She comes to my bed, kisses my chin. "Think about where you'd like us to go tomorrow."

"I don't care. All the snowdrops are gone by now."

"We'll look for violets. And there are willows blooming by the river."

I turn to the wall.

She takes my hand, pinches my fingertips, one by one. "Hello there, Exordimus. You're looking good, Princess Exilobí. How are you doing, Auntie Chalupka . . . ?"

Añañaña, Atlonvévev. Silly names we made up for my fingers when I was little.

I laugh into my pillow, then turn, to hug her.

DEAR EVA

April 15, 1942

Dear Eva,

You said I *must* write about Aunt Lena's wedding. There wasn't any. She went out with Uncle Teo for a while and came back married. NO music. NO dancing. Some grownups came in the evening to drink wine and eat poppy-seed cake Aunt Lena baked. It was boring. I stayed up till ten.

Uncle Teo's house is gray. It has a red tile roof. A big chestnut tree in front of the house covers part of the roof. In the garden, just outside my window, is a walnut tree that's easy to climb. When I wake up mornings I watch birds hopping from branch to branch and sharpening their beaks.

The garden is big. When you come visit we'll play hide-and-seek. We can hide behind the currant and gooseberry bushes. In the woodshed are lots of secret places for hiding, too.

Excuse the ink spots. This nib stinks. I need a new one.

> Love, love, love
> Katarína

P.S. Tomorrow I'll be getting my first letter from you.

> April 16

Dear Eva,

I ran home from school to read your letter, but it didn't get here yet. I have to wait till tomorrow.

Our teacher is Miss Sipková. I like her very much. The teacher for embroidery has a big mouth and shouts a lot. The girls call her Dragon Lady.

I share my desk with Božena. Her father is a policeman. There are two policemen in this village. Božena is nice, but she is not my best friend, like you.

Uncle Teo's son, Pavel, has dark blue eyes and blond hair, like Aunt Lena. He works in a sawmill down the river and comes home only on weekends. Last Sunday he took me to the Orava River (it flows by this village, too) and showed me how to skip stones. He can make his stones skip five, six times. Mine sink as soon as they hit the water.

It was cold. When we got home, Aunt Lena made us hot chocolate and heated water for a bath.

I still have homework to do. Lots of love,

> Katarína

April 17

Dear Eva,

Your letter still didn't get here. This is my third letter. Did you get letters one and two?

I showed Miss Sipková a poem I wrote. It's about the Orava River and the mountains I see from my window. It says how beautiful Slovakia is. Miss Sipková said the poem was very good. She is sending it to *Sunrise* so that children in the whole country can read it. Our school gets the magazine on Tuesdays, same as yours.

We have a new maid. Her name is Anka. She is seventeen. Her hair is down to her shoulders and shines like gold. She doesn't talk to me much. She is stuck-up.

Love,
Katarína

P.S. Did you remember to put a stamp on the envelope?

April 18

Dear Eva,

We promised to write every day. Why don't you? Are you very busy?

I miss you. Aunt Lena doesn't have much time for me. She is always cooking, baking, or typing documents in Uncle Teo's office. When she and he have secrets from me they talk in Hungarian, like last night. They don't know I understand almost everything they're saying.

When Aunt Lena and I lived in Bratislava, a Hungarian family moved into the apartment downstairs. They didn't speak Slovak. I played with their daughters, Ilonka and Irenka, and learned a lot of Hungarian.

You once asked me why we left Bratislava. Aunt Lena says we had to, because Hitler wanted the capital of Slovakia *Judenrein*. That means, clean of Jews. Also, because she lost her job. Her boss said she was a Communist.

Love,
Katarína

P.S. Bratislava has the tallest house in the world—it's *eleven* stories high. Someday, when we're older, I'll show it to you. I'll also show you where I was born; it's the house where Ilonka and Irenka live. We can visit them.

April 19

Dear Eva,

Yesterday I forgot to write why Aunt Lena and Uncle Teo talked in Hungarian the night before.

I keep asking my aunt to let me go to Hlinka Youth meetings. Božena tells me they learn songs and dances, play games, march, and listen to stories about Slovak heroes. Tomorrow they're having a BIG birthday party for Adolf Hitler. He won't be there. Božena said I could come even if I'm not a member yet. I asked Aunt Lena, and that's when she and Uncle Teo started talking (SHOUTING!) in Hungarian.

He said, "Yes, the child should go"—he always calls me *the child*!—"It's good if she's seen there, good for her, good for us, blah . . . blah . . . blah . . ." Aunt Lena said, "I won't allow it, Teo, there are limits, the very idea is blah . . . blah . . ." I didn't understand all the words, but enough to know that Uncle Teo was on *my* side. In the end she agreed to let me go with Božena to the next regular meeting but NOT to Hitler's birthday party.

Eva, please, please, write. Much love,

Katarína

April 22, 1942

Dear Eva,

Every day I run to meet the mail truck. No letter from you yet. This is letter number six. Are you sick?

Yesterday Božena came over to play. Uncle Teo made us go outside, in the rain. Aunt Lena says he isn't used to children in the house anymore. He writes important documents and needs to concentrate, she says.

When you visit, you'll see Uncle Teo's waiting room. It's the funniest. The peasants don't have much money. They pay with things from their farms, like eggs, butter, cheese, bacon, ham. They also bring chickens, roosters, geese, turkeys, ducks, *alive*. While they're waiting, little feathery heads

keep popping out of baskets and bundles from behind their backs. Sometimes the honks, quacks,
cackles, cock-a-doodle-doos get so loud that Uncle
Teo comes running out of his office. "Quiet! I can't
think," he shouts. "What is this, a barnyard?"

There's no more ink in this bottle, I have to st

April 23

Dear Eva,

I think I know what happened to your letters. The
postmistress is keeping them because I'm new here
and she doesn't know who Katarína is. Or else she
gave the letters to another Katarina in this village, by
mistake. I am running to find out.

Love,
Katarína

P.S. The post office was closed. The note on the door
said, 'Tomáš's grandchild due today. Post office
opens again tomorrow, God willing.' Tomáš is the
baker in this village. Aunt Lena says the postmistress
is also the village midwife.

More love,
Katarína

April 24

Eva!

I went to the post office straight from school. No
letters for Katarína came to this village. I am *really*

mad at you. You broke your promise to write to me every day. You are a lazy stinker. I don't want you to write any letters. If you do, I won't read them. I'll send them back.

Katarína

April 25

Dear Eva,

Tear up the letter I sent you yesterday into a hundred little pieces. I am very, *very* sorry I got mad at you. I didn't mean anything I said. You are my best friend. I love you very much.

Katarína

P.S. On my way home from school I picked a bunch of forget-me-nots and tossed them into the river. I said, "Here, Orava, take these flowers to Eva." I think you are now best friends with Kristína.

April 28

Dear Eva,

You won't believe this. Someone brought Uncle Teo a baby pig. It was snorting in a basket, its legs tied, when suddenly it got loose and started running down the hall. Anka and the peasant who brought it and I chased it while Aunt Lena rushed to close all the doors in the house. Anka caught it. The poor thing wouldn't stop squealing. Uncle Teo told the man to take "that animal" back to his farm, we had no place to keep it. I was sorry. The piglet was so pink, so clean, I would have made space for it in my room.

Love,
Katarína

May 1

Dear Eva,

Don't forget my birthday this month. How lucky the sixteenth falls on a Saturday. No school—you can come.

Anka and I got up early today to see which roof had the highest maypole. The night before, we made a bet. I thought Poluška's would—she is the prettiest girl in the village. Anka bet on the mayor's daughter because she's the richest.

We were both wrong. The tallest and most beautiful maypole was on Miss Sipková's roof. It had hundreds of long ribbons and streamers, mostly red, swirling around the pole. Sometimes the wind would chase them, drive them away from the pole as far as they could stretch, but then they'd rush right back, to hug it. Anka and I wonder who loves Miss Sipková so very much. She'll be embarrassed in class because we will tease her, especially the boys.

Forget that I said Anka was stuck-up. She's the nicest. Her parents and younger brothers and sisters live on a farm. Anka said she'll take me there, on her days off, as soon as school lets out. Aunt Lena said I could go.

Love,
Katarína

May 4

Dear Eva,

I don't know if you got my letters. Maybe they're lost, or your mom doesn't let you read them.

Yesterday, Sunday, Anka took me to Mass. I am now Catholic. Tell your mom, so she'll let you come for my birthday. There's a bus that gets here Saturdays at noon. I'll wait for you at the bus stop.

Love,
Katarína

P.S. Don't forget to look for my poem in *Sunrise* magazine tomorrow.

May 7

Dear Eva,

This is *very* important.

Aunt Lena knows that I go to Mass with Anka, but she doesn't know that every night, after she and Uncle Teo go to bed, Anka tells me stories about the saints and teaches me lessons from the catechism. Be sure you don't mention a word about it when you're here on Saturday.

Love,
Katarína

P.S. Tell Kristína she can come to my birthday party, too.

May 9

Dear Eva,

I went to a Hlinka Youth meeting with Božena. Our group leader has yellow teeth and they're so long they stick out of her mouth. She said I could come again as Božena's guest, but to be a member I need to get a stamped card from the Central Office.

We learned a song about brave Hlinka Youth maidens, and then we marched in the village square, shouting, "Long live Tiso! Long live Tuka!" Tuka is very important in the government; he is the Prime Minister.

Our principal, Vojtech Rospačil, says that all Slovak children should be proud to wear the Hlinka Youth uniform. I asked Aunt Lena to get me one for my birthday.

Love,
Katarína

P.S. I am trying out for a part in a school play. Keep your fingers crossed I get it.

May 12, 1942

Dear Eva,

I'll tell you the biggest secret ever if you promise to forget it and tear up this letter as soon as you read it.

I love Uncle Teo's son, Pavel. When I grow up I will marry him.

Don't say a word about it to Kristína. And don't giggle when you see Pavel on Saturday. May Saint Ján of Nepomuk keep your lips sealed.

Remember Aunt Lena's rule—no birthday presents. Only four days until I see you.

Love,
Katarína

P.S. Thank you for keeping your fingers crossed. Miss Sipková chose me to be the Dancing Orchid in our play.

P.S.S. My poem wasn't in this week's *Sunrise* either. Did you look for it?

May 17

Eva!

You missed the best birthday party, ever.
I will never invite you again.
This is *definitely* and *positively* my LAST letter.

Katarína

May 20

This is NOT a letter. Just to tell you you're not my friend anymore. Now I will tell my secrets to Božena.

SAINTS

Every night I tiptoe to Anka's room. She tells me stories about the Infant Jesus, the Holy Virgin, about the saints whose feast day it is. Today, June 13, is Saint Anton's.

It all started when I circled on our kitchen calendar the date of my eighth birthday.

"That's a very special day, Katarínka," she said.

"It is. My best friend, Eva, is coming, I'll get to stay up late, Aunt Lena will bake my favorite chocolate cake—"

"That's not why it's special, you silly. May 16 is the feast day of Saint Ján of Nepomuk."

"Is he very important?"

"He used to be the patron saint of our country, when it was Czechoslovakia. That was before the war."

"And he isn't anymore? Did saints lose their jobs because of the war, like the Jews and the Communists?"

"We Slovaks have our own country now and our own patron saint, and the Czechs have theirs. But Saint Ján is still important. I pray to him every time I cross a bridge. And at other times, too."

"A bridge? Why?"

"Katarína, I am busy. I have to get wood from the shed and start the fire for supper. Ask me later."

Later, she was cleaning up the kitchen and I was sent to bed. When the last light in the house went out, I knocked on her door.

"What are you doing here, Katarína?"

"You promised, Anka. You said you'd tell me why you pray to Saint Ján every time you cross a bridge."

"I'll tell you tomorrow."

"Tomorrow you'll be busy."

She sighed and pointed to her only chair. "All right, sit down."

Anka's room is small. There is the narrow bed she was sitting on, a dresser, a wardrobe, and a small table. The walls are covered with pictures of saints. A large wooden cross hangs over her bed.

"What I'm about to tell you happened about six hundred years ago. That's when Ján was born, in the town of Nepomuk, near Prague."

The only light in the room came from the moon. Anka lit a candle, then reached for a pack of cards on her cluttered dresser. They were pictures of saints.

On the first card she showed me was a man dressed like a priest. Above his head were seven stars. On the second, the same man was standing on a bridge, looking at the river. The third picture showed him holding his finger to his lips. In his other hand was a padlock.

"What's the padlock for, Anka?"

"Ján was a priest and the confessor of the king's wife, Sofie. The king wanted Ján to tell him Sofie's secrets, but Ján wouldn't, not even under torture. That's why he is the patron saint of secrets as well as of bridges."

"Why of bridges?"

"The king wanted to appoint a favorite of his as head of an abbey. Everybody knew the king's choice was wrong— his favorite was someone unworthy—but no one had the courage to oppose the king, except Ján of Nepomuk. The king got so angry he tortured Ján with a burning torch. Then he had him gagged, tied to a wheel, and thrown off the bridge into the Vltava River. That night seven bright stars hovered over the spot where Ján drowned."

All the next day I kept thinking about Saint Ján and the miracle of the seven stars and what it was like to be tortured. At night I sneaked out of bed and went to Anka's room again. I wanted to hear more about the saints. She told me the story of Saint Katarína. "A princess . . ." Anka said. "Beautiful. Strong. Wise. She wouldn't marry anyone, not even the king, because she was betrothed to Jesus. 'Torture me on that wheel all you want,' she told the king. 'It won't change my mind.'

"Saint Katarína is watching over you, Katarínka; she is your patron saint. Pray to her when you're in trouble. You can also ask her for special favors."

"Can I ask her to get rid of my freckles?"

"Hmmmmm—I don't know. God made you with freckles. Saint Katarína wouldn't want to interfere."

"But I hate them! Everyone in class makes fun of me."

"Ask Old Krasovka. She'll help you."

"Go to her? Oh, no. I saw that ugly witch up close, at the cemetery. Suddenly, there she was, crouched behind a tombstone."

"She's not a witch. Old Krasovka knows secrets about plants, birds, and other things we don't know. She'll work up some magic for your freckles if you take her a sausage or two."

"I'm scared of her. Božena swears she's a witch."

"Krasovka helped a woman from my village. Made her warts disappear overnight."

"No, no. I'd rather ask Saint Katarína." How lucky I am, I thought, to be her namesake.

"Tell me about Saint Anton. Today is his feast day."

"No stories tonight, Katarínka. Sit down."

There is something different about Anka tonight. She is pale and her mouth is drawn in a tight, thin line. The cross that hangs from a golden chain around her neck quivers on her embroidered linen blouse.

"You must never tell anyone what you're about to hear."

"I won't, Anka."

"Swear it on the picture of Ján of Nepomuk. On this one, with the padlock."

"I swear."

"May he keep your lips sealed."

She sits down next to me, on the bed, takes my hand, and holds it between hers.

"Two nights ago I had a dream." She is talking softly,

slowly, as if she were still dreaming. "It was about you. You were a little lamb, crying—"

"How do you know the lamb was me?"

"Be quiet, listen. I know it was you. The lamb was crying, looking for the path it lost—"

"Did it find the path?"

"I don't know. I woke up." Anka stops talking. It is quiet in the room except for the hiss the dripping wax makes each time a droplet falls on the copper plate under the candle. Was that all Anka had to tell me, I wonder. What is so special about her dream that she made me swear on a picture of Saint Ján?

"Katarína—last night I experienced a vision."

I stared at her. "*A vision?* What did you see, where?"

"Here, in my room. The Blessed Mother—"

"The Blessed Mother came to this house? You saw her, in your room?"

"I didn't see her, not exactly, but she was here. I always know when she is with me. I feel it."

"What do you feel? What's it like?"

"There's silence, then a sound like the rustle of silk . . . I feel dizzy, hot and cold at the same time . . . gooseflesh creeps up my arms but my palms are sweating . . . and then, last night for the first time, I heard a voice . . ."

My kneecaps are jumping. I pull Anka's bedcovers up around me. "What did the voice tell you?"

"It told me to save you. To show you the true path. I didn't want to come work in a Jewish home, but something told me I had to. Now I understand. Jesus wants me here."

"But, Anka, I've been Catholic ever since you first took me to Sunday Mass."

"Going to church on Sundays isn't enough to make you Catholic. You need to know the prayers, study the catechism, learn about the Holy Trinity, the fifteen mysteries, the Sacraments—and most important, Katarína, you have to believe in the Son of God, our Saviour—"

"Oh, but I do, Anka, I believe in Jesus, I *do*!"

Anka has bought me a rosary and picture cards of saints, like the packet she has. I hide them inside a woolen stocking, in my dresser. She teaches me Catholic prayers and songs, tests me on answers I memorize from the catechism, tells me about saints and the visions they had. The candlelight makes me drowsy—sometimes I fall asleep in Anka's bed and tiptoe back to mine only at dawn, when the rooster wakes us.

I like being Catholic—it's cheerful having all those saints around to talk to.

Whenever I lose my bracelet or misplace my eraser, Saint Anton helps me find them.

My embroidery stitches are neater ever since I've been getting help from Saint Klára.

Saint Beňadik cured my nettle rash, Saint Vít protects me from lightning.

When Aunt Lena has a headache, I pray to Saint Štefan for her. On Tuesday nights Anka and I pray together to Saint Marta. We ask her to turn the dough Aunt Lena prepared into a loaf of bread she'd be proud of.

THE SECRET

Those geese under my window belong to Božena's parents. I recognize the gray gander in the lead and the goose that limps at a distance cackling, cackling, lest she be forgotten and left behind. Božena's little brother must be here. It's his job to mind the geese.

"Jura!"

He's nowhere to be seen.

I lean out of the window. "Jura!"

Something drops from a tree. He is barefoot though it's late September, and his nose is running.

"Whadya want?"

"Tell Božena to meet me at the cemetery when they ring for vespers. Hurry."

Jura doesn't move. The rascal. May corn grow out of his ears!

I rush to the kitchen. Clothes are piled on chairs, empty knapsacks lie scattered on the floor, rows of canned food line the table. I can hardly squeeze through.

"Can't you sleep?" my aunt asks.

"No, I'm not used to sleeping in the afternoon. May I take an apple?"

In the dark pantry I grope for walnuts inside the burlap bag and fill my pockets. I also take an apple and a fistful of raisins.

Jura stares at the walnuts.

"Here, take two. I'll send the rest with Božena."

Jura leaves the geese and runs to deliver my message.

I lie down on my bed and wait for the vesper bell. A meeting at the cemetery means that Božena or I have an important secret. Today, the secret is mine.

"I have something to tell you," Aunt Lena had said to me when I came home from school. "It is very serious."

I studied my aunt's face for a clue, but her expression was one I had never seen before.

"Uncle Teo lost his exemption from President Tiso. He can no longer work as a lawyer and we could be deported."

"Is there another roundup?"

"The roundups continued through the spring and the summer. But until now we were protected."

"But Uncle Teo is old, and you'll be thirty next month. Will they still want you in the work camps?"

"They're taking everybody. Children, old people—the couple down the street—"

"That ancient Jewish couple you said moved somewhere else—they went to the camp?"

"Yes, Katinka."

"Why didn't they hide if they didn't want to go?"

"It's not that easy, Katarína. You have to know people who are kind and brave enough to take the risk, or pay someone a lot of money. The couple had no warning. The Hlinka Guard knocked on their door and took them away."

"Does Uncle Teo have money?"

"We're lucky. He has money and we were warned. Late tonight Husár, a farmer, will take us through back roads to another village—about an hour's walk from here—and he will hide us in his barn."

Barn? My heart skipped with joy. I had not done one additional stitch on my embroidery, and now I wouldn't have to face the Dragon Lady. Instead of cringing in my seat, I'll be jumping off a ladder into piles of hay.

"You are not to leave the house anymore. If any of your classmates—Božena, Karla, or Terka—show up, I'll send them away. You are not to talk to anyone. This is very serious. Do you understand?"

"U-hm . . ." I was thinking of how to arrange a meeting with Božena.

"I'll pack a knapsack with things you'll need and you can add a few—colored pencils, notepaper, some games, a couple of books—nothing very bulky or heavy."

"What about Anka and Pavel? Are they coming, too?"

"Anka will help out your teacher, Miss Sipková, while we're gone, and Pavel doesn't have to hide. He has an exemption because of his work at the sawmill."

"When will we come back?"

"I don't know. Don't bother me or Uncle Teo with questions. Go to your room and try to sleep. I'll wake you when it's time to leave."

"Next week are the tryouts for our new school play. Will we be back?"

"Katinka . . ." She started to say something but stopped. She looked so sad I thought she would cry.

The vesper bell! It startles me, though I've been waiting for it. I lock my door from the inside, then jump out the window.

The shortcut: over the hedge, through the hole in Radko's fence, across the pasture—quick, before the bull sees me—past Uncle Dodák's orchard—the apples are turning color, they'll soon be ripe for picking—and instead of taking the bridge, I skip from rock to rock across the stream, run up the hill, and reach the cemetery at the last stroke of the bell.

Božena is there, waiting.

"Quick!" I whisper. "They don't know I'm out."

"What about me?" She pouts. "I'm supposed to be churning butter."

"It's very important. The biggest secret ever."

Božena's eyes glitter with excitement.

These are our rules: big secrets may be shared only on the hilltop behind the cemetery chapel. There we draw the magic circle. Inside the circle we are under oath to speak the truth and not keep anything from each other. The circle's magic power also keeps spirits away—

they're apt to eavesdrop and gossip. And should one of us betray a confidence, she would come under an evil spell.

"You could turn into a hedgehog, like Fučík, the night watchman," Božena had warned me, "or into a bat! Remember when the tinker's mother-in-law disappeared for a month? Old Krasovka punished her for blabbing. Turned her into a goat."

Božena's world is full of magic. She trips on a rock and shakes her fist at a gnome only she can see. She overturns the milk bucket and chases an imp with her broom. She speaks with little demons that sit on fences and sticks out her tongue at a raven—she knows who it *really* is. When we decided to become friends, she led me to the hilltop behind the chapel, and drew a circle. Inside that circle we swore love and loyalty to each other, forever.

I follow Božena up the hill. Her braid is tied with a string—she wears ribbons only on Sundays.

"Is it about Pavel?"

"No."

Božena knows I love Pavel; it's one of the big secrets I confessed behind the chapel. Another time I told her about the kiss. Pavel never paid much attention to me, but one day, suddenly, he lifted me in his arms and kissed me on the nose. It happened the day he got that exemption paper from the sawmill.

We pass the chapel and reach the top of the hill. Božena picks up a sharp-edged rock.

"Here. You draw it!"

I trace a circle on the ground while she chants:

> "Magic circle, evil spell,
>   guard our secret, guard it well.
>   Let no other human ear
>   Katarína's secret hear,
>   and if I should talk and tell
>   may I die and roast in hell."

We step inside the circle. Božena's face is like an empty bowl that wants to be filled.

My throat tightens. I shiver, fumble in my pockets. The walnuts. I forgot about them. "Here," I tell Božena. "These are for Jura."

She slips them into the slit pockets of her wide peasant skirt.

"Well?"

What's happened? I was so eager to tell her my secret, and now the words sit in my throat like lumps of stale bread.

"Tell me!"

"Yes . . . just a minute."

A swallow chirps overhead. I follow its flight across the red sky over the rooftops of the village: there is the school, there the post office, and next to it the smithy. I retrace my steps over the brook, past Dodák's orchard, across Radko's pasture, and over the fence to the gray stone house with its red-tiled roof partly hidden by the chestnut tree. Inside, my aunt and uncle are packing knapsacks. I see the worried look on Aunt Lena's face, hear her voice: "You are not to talk to anyone . . . This is very serious . . . Do you understand?" Was this a secret not to be shared even with Božena?

I look at my red-cheeked friend, a Hlinka Youth member and daughter of the village policeman. She is staring at me intently, her expression changing from curiosity to impatience.

"What is it? You've lost your tongue?"

From the flurry of strange feelings that have overcome me I begin to understand something. But understanding only makes it worse.

"Božena . . ."

"Yes?"

"Božena, I . . . I cannot talk about this, to anyone!"

She nods. "Sure! Only I will know."

"No. I mean . . . I can't share this secret with anyone in the whole world!" I swallow hard and whisper, "Not even with you."

"What's that? You brought me up here just to make a fool of me?"

"Oh, no! I meant to tell you, I really did, but now I know that I can't."

"Why? Why not?"

I cannot look at her or answer her.

"But I'm your friend, Katarína. We share all of our secrets, we always do!"

I long to tell her. I feel as if a current were sweeping me into waters too deep, and telling Božena my secret would bring me back to shore.

"You must tell me! We're inside the magic circle— you're under oath!"

I'm shivering, but my palms are moist with sweat.

She stamps her foot. "For the last time, will you tell me, or not?"

"I can't."

Božena glares at me. "I'm not your friend anymore," she shouts. "I hate you!"

She whirls around and darts down the hill.

I want to call after her, ask her to come back, but all I do is watch her get smaller and farther away.

Below, the village is disappearing under a thin gray veil; here and there a light flickers . . . black smoke curls from chimneys before it, too, blends into the gray.

Standing inside the magic circle, I listen to the bells and the bellowing of cows coming back from pasture, the cracking of the cowherd's whip. I hear geese honking, mothers calling their children home, ox-drawn carts rumbling along unpaved roads.

The first stars appear. Now the village is silent. It is potato harvest time, when peasant families eat their meals out in the fields, around open fires. The scents of burning wood, of earth, of roasting potatoes linger in the air and mingle with the scent of ripening apples, of fresh-cut grass, of herbs growing on the hillsides . . .

It's getting late. I ought to run home as fast as I can. But I don't. Something is keeping me moored to the spot.

Are Božena's imps and demons punishing me for not sharing my secret?

I cannot step out of the magic circle.

THE HUSÁRS' BARN

Through cracks in the Husárs' barn wall I can watch the village boys play soccer.

The meadow where they play is just below our hiding place. I need only move close to the wall and squint through the space between the boards. I am getting to know the players.

There is Anton. He runs the fastest. Štefan has the strongest legs but often kicks the ball to the wrong team, or up so high it spins level with my nose. Durik, the Husárs' son, cheats. From here I can see him trip other players and hear him swear that he doesn't. Viktor, the oldest, tries to break up fights between the teams.

Today is Sunday. On Sundays all the girls and boys too young to play come to cheer for their teams. Ignác the half-wit claps his hands and shrieks each time a goal is scored. His legs are stumps that end at the knees. He stretches his arms and strains to touch the ball as it speeds over his head.

Little Miruško is crying because he is too young to

join a team. He kicks and flails while his big sister tries to wipe his face with her petticoat.

Under the linden tree lazy Matúš and his dog lie sleeping. It is a warm afternoon. Very warm for October.

"Aunt Lena, what time is it?"

"Quiet! You've been told a thousand times to *whisper*!"

I whisper, "What time is it, please?"

She points to her watch. "Three minutes went by since you last asked."

"Only three minutes? I'm going crazy!"

"Did you finish *The Prince and the Pauper*?"

"Yes. Five times."

"Memorize the next chapter of *Maya the Bee*. You did so well with the first three."

"I'm bored with *Maya*!"

"Then how about memorizing another poem?"

"They're all silly!"

She sighs. How can she lie so still under that heap of hay, for days, only her head and eyes moving?

"Aunt Lena, why did the soccer games stop?"

"I don't know. It's been raining."

"But it isn't raining today!"

"The meadow must be muddy."

"No, it's not, I can see from here. Look!"

"Katinka, be quiet. Take a nap. Or visit with Igor."

I glance at the corner beam above my head. Igor isn't at home. He must be tired of my watching him. He is probably spinning a new web somewhere else. Or crawling under my blanket. Or in Uncle Teo's new beard.

"I can't nap in the afternoon."

She sighs again. "Let's play twenty questions. Think of something, or someone."

"Not that stupid game again. Let's think of a new one. Or tell me a story. You started one yesterday. What happened when—"

"Keep that child quiet, Lena, or *I'll* go crazy!"

Uncle Teo's whisper sounds like a hiss. Some days he loses all patience with me. Not that he has much to start with. Aunt Lena lies between us to keep him from taping my mouth shut, as he threatens to.

I wouldn't nap even if I could. When I do, I can't sleep at night and nighttime moves even *more* slowly. Nothing to watch, no one to talk to. All those spooky sounds and Aunt Lena asleep, close to Uncle Teo. Too far for me to touch when I want to.

"Aunt Lena, how come it's so dark?"

"It's November. The days are getting shorter."

That means longer nights. More spook sounds, rat squeaks, scary faces that in the morning turn out to be a knapsack or a paper bag. More time for wishing the night were over.

"Aunt Lena . . ."

She gives me a warning look.

It couldn't be any worse in a work camp. We'd be outdoors, moving about, talking as much, as loud, as we wanted. We could shout. Sing. I bet they sing and tell stories evenings around a bonfire. And after a day's work we'd sleep right through the night. No scary sounds and faces, no choking on hay dust, no thrashing about to get at insect bites. The work couldn't be that hard. Not as hard as lying here day after day, night after night, with nothing to do but count minutes that never move ahead.

I tug Aunt Lena's sleeve. I ask my question with the finger alphabet we made up a few days ago.

She holds up her wrist for me to see.

Only five minutes have passed.

The wind blows through the cracks between the boards of the barn wall.

We stacked our knapsacks against the boards, stuffed the spaces between them with newspaper, and still the wind comes through. We are wearing caps, gloves, and shawls; we burrow deeper into the hay, but my teeth keep chattering.

"Aunt Lena, how will we know when the war is over?"

"We'll hear the church bells. All the church bells will be ringing."

"We have to stay here till it's over? Spend Christmas *here*?"

"No, Katinka. We'll be going home before then."

"Soon?"

No answer. That means not soon. And it'll keep getting colder!

"I want a sugar wafer."

"There are none left."

"Not a *one?*"

She shakes her head.

"Where is the box of crackers?"

Uncle Teo sits up. "Is the child really hungry or just bored?" Aunt Lena shrugs. She doesn't know. Neither do I.

"Explain to her, Lena, that we must ration our food. She has not understood that yet!"

"Let her have the crackers, Teo. Pavel comes with fresh supplies tomorrow."

"And if he can't? Do I need to explain to you, too, that there is a war?"

Aunt Lena reaches for the box of crackers and hands me two. I chew them with an open mouth to annoy Uncle Teo. The crackers are salty and dry. They make me thirsty.

"Where are you going?"

"I want to get a drink and then to pee. Come with me, Aunt Lena, *please.*"

She listens for voices, for footsteps. It's quiet. We can move.

We crawl to the edge of the alcove, to the water pail. I blow aside the drowned insects and bits of hay before I dip in the ladle. Husár and Husárka, his wife, change the water when they happen to remember.

They also empty the stinky slop pail. It is on the other end of the narrow tunnel, so narrow that we have to slither on our bellies. Pavel dug the tunnel through the hay the third or fourth time he brought us supplies. It was my aunt's idea.

"We need the privacy," she said. "We can't live like pigs."

"We have to," Uncle Teo argued. "Crawling to the pail over there will make too much noise."

"Teo, we need this bit of dignity or else all this isn't worth it!"

Uncle Teo gave in. He held the flashlight while Pavel dug. Aunt Lena thanked them. "A belated birthday present," she whispered. "One I'll never forget." We all hugged her. No one had remembered her birthday.

Now we have our privacy, but I am afraid of choking. I take a deep breath and hold it until I get to the other side. Sometimes it feels as if I won't make it through. That's why I want Aunt Lena to come with me, to make sure I don't get stuck in there or chewed up by a rat.

I like the side opposite our alcove. There is no hay, only bare floorboards. I can stand up. Stretch. Walk! It's five steps to the pail.

Aunt Lena comes out of the tunnel covered with hay. "You look funny." I laugh at her. "A walking haystack."

"Quiet, Katinka, they'll hear us!"

The Husárs prop a ladder on our side when they bring us water for drinking and brushing teeth. They no longer carry up buckets for washing. We clean ourselves with cotton balls dipped in rubbing alcohol.

To empty the slop pail, the Husárs move the ladder to the other side, and when they're done they lock it up somewhere so no one else can climb it.

. . .

"One, two, three, four, five, six, seven, eight . . ."

The Husár children and their friends are playing hide-and-seek. The one who is "it" counts to twenty while the others hide. Veročka and Jolanka, the youngest Husár daughters, are looking for a hiding place inside the barn.

"Here. This is a good spot. Cover me with hay and find some other place for yourself."

"Where?"

"Anywhere!"

"There is no anywhere. I want to stay with you!"

"Hey, look!"

"What?"

"The ladder's back. You stay here. I'll go up there!"

Uncle Teo gasps. He points to what we didn't notice before: two wooden horns, the tips of the ladder, peering over the edge of our alcove. Once again Husárka forgot to take it away!

"Mother says we're not to go up there."

"She won't know."

"She'll punish us if she finds out."

"Oh, hush! I'm going."

Uncle Teo looks at Aunt Lena. His eyes are begging her to stop Veročka, but there is nothing Aunt Lena can do. The ladder horns quiver. My uncle motions us to lie still, then slides forward and sits cross-legged between the tips of the ladder. The last thing I see him do is toss an armful of hay over his head.

A scream.

Shriek follows shriek. Footsteps scramble down the ladder.

"S-save me, sweet Jesus, save me!"

"Veročka, what's got into you? Are you crazy?"

"There's a man up there with straw growing out of his head—"

"What?"

"—and huge, enormous eyes. I swear!"

Uncle Teo points to his spectacles—the huge, enormous eyes Veročka saw.

All the children are inside the barn, asking questions. "What happened?" "Why was she screaming?" "What did she see up there?" Veročka is crying.

"She says there's a man up there with straw growing out of his head!"

"A strawman! Our Veročka saw a strawman up in the alcove."

That is Durik talking.

"I'll have a look," he says. "Anyone coming up with me?"

Uncle Teo's face is the color of milk. His mouth hangs open. Once again the wooden horns quiver. We freeze.

"Hey, what are you all doing here? Get out, at once!"

Husárka's high-pitched voice rises above the children's.

"There's a man up there, Mama, I saw—"

"Get down, Durik, or I'll thrash you, big as you are!"

From the way the tips are clanging against the boards,

she must be shaking the ladder. A thud. Durik must have jumped, or fallen.

"Now out! All of you!"

The barn clears. We can hear Veročka, still stammering from fright, telling her mother what she saw.

Uncle Teo shakes his head. "That's it. By evening the whole village will know."

"No one will take her seriously, Teo. Little children imagine things."

"Durik is old enough to catch on. The girl sees a 'strawman,' the mother is hysterical, a ladder's kept under lock and key—the boy would be stupid not to suspect something."

"Calm down, Teo. We can't leave."

"We have to. Husárka can't be trusted. That ladder's been there all morning, anyone could have come up."

"Teo, we have no place to go."

"But we *do*," I almost shout, then remember to whisper. "We do have a place to go." I roll over my aunt and wedge myself between them. "Please, Uncle Teo, please, Aunt Lena, let's go to that work camp. We'd be outdoors. There'd be bathrooms instead of stinky slop pails. I could play with other children and not annoy you all day. I'm sick of lying still, sick of whispering and crawling. I want us to go to the camp."

Aunt Lena sighs. "Child, you don't know what you're saying."

"I do. I want to go. We're rotting here just because you're too lazy to work. I hate you!"

Uncle Teo stares at me.

Aunt Lena covers her face with her palms.

I make up my mind: the next time Durik comes inside the barn I'll scream.

Children are coming down the mountain path carrying buckets filled with berries: blueberries, raspberries, huckleberries, strawberries . . .

Pink, red, and purple juices color their bare feet as they crush the berries spilled on the path. Ignác the half-wit strains to touch the fruit-filled buckets bouncing past us.

"You there. Get a pail and join us. There are berries to pick."

"Lift the pine branches off the ground. You'll find mushrooms big as a fist."

"I can't."

"What did she say?"

"Don't know. Can't hear her."

"Hey, speak up."

"I'm not allowed to. They'll hear me."

"What?"

A young man stoops down to listen to me. It is Viktor. He is grownup, with a mustache.

"Who is they?"

"You know. The war. They're looking for us."

"The war?" Viktor slaps his thigh, laughing. "The war's long over. You don't have to whisper. You can shout."

I open my mouth to shout, but what comes out of my throat is a choked rasp.

"Toss her a pail, Štefan. Come on, summer won't stay forever."

A pail rolls down the slope. I stretch my arms but cannot reach it.

"Hurry up, it's getting late."

I stare into the white, empty pail. The sun sets behind the mountains. The pail turns gray. I keep trying to reach it. All the children are gone except Ignác. He claps his hands and shrieks. In the darkness I grope for the pail I can no longer see.

Feet. Running, tripping each other, changing directions. Feet of children playing soccer. There is Anton, quicker than the others. There is Durik, tripping Štefan. Ignác, rising on his stumps, tries to touch the ball as it speeds over his head.

"Hey, you, come play with us."

Me? He means me, a girl? He must. Ignác and I are the only ones here.

"What are you waiting for?"

I know that boy. It's Miruško, now old enough to play on a team.

"I can't," I whisper, hiding the stumps that are my legs.

"She's still whispering. She doesn't believe us."

"You hear those bells?" lazy Matúš shouts from under the linden tree. "The war's over, that's why they're ringing."

"Aunt Lena, is that true?"

Where is she? She was sitting beside me just now, embroidering.

"Uncle Teo"—I turn to him—"is that true?"

Strands of hay grow out of his head. Hay dribbles from his mouth. Spiders crawl in his empty eyes. I want to run, but my legs won't hold me.

Miruško bounces the soccer ball. "Get up by the time I count to ten or we'll never let you play with us. You hear?"

"Yes."

"One, two, three . . ."

The bells keep ringing. Their sound fills the valley.

I cling to the sound as if it were a rope and try to pull myself up.

"Four, five, six, seven . . ."

"Stop, I can't!"

"You what? Eight, nine . . ."

"I can't, I caaaaan't!"

A hand covers my mouth.

The head of Ignác the half-wit is a soccer ball spinning round, round, round . . .

"Wake up, Katinka. You're having a bad dream."

Aunt Lena is rubbing my forehead, breaking up the nightmare. The children and the meadow are gone. But the bells keep ringing.

"Aunt Lena, those bells . . ."

"What about them?"

"Is the war over?"

"No."

"Then why are they ringing?"

"It's Christmas, Katinka. They're ringing for midnight Mass."

I press my forehead against the icy boards and peer at the moonlit landscape.

As far as I can see, lanterns flicker on footpaths cleared between walls of snow. From all parts of the village people are walking to church.

Midnight Mass. Inside the church it is warm. It is bright. I wish I were there, with Anka; she told me what it's like. A thousand candles light up the altar. Colored glass windows sparkle, golden halos glow. Priests and altar boys in festive vestments walk down the aisle swinging incense burners. The fragrant smoke circles the heads of the bundled-up, red-cheeked peasants, then rises to turn into little white clouds. Saints in niches along the walls look as if they're stirring, about to step onto the clouds at their feet. The organ plays softly during prayers. Then, like a peacock spreading its tail, it swells with sounds so strong, so beautiful, they make you shiver. The church is full of music—the organ, the ringing of bells, and at midnight, singing, too, as worshippers greet our Saviour, the Infant Jesus—"Silent night, holy night . . ."

"You're shivering. Get back under the blankets."

"You said we wouldn't be spending Christmas here!"

I look at Aunt Lena. In the moonlight her skin looks yellow. Her cheeks are hollow, her eyes sunken and dull. Something sharp turns in my belly. I crawl under the blankets and burrow deep into the hay.

"After the war, may I go pick berries with the other children?"

She doesn't answer. I curl up so tightly that my knees meet my chin.

"And when the war is over," I whisper, "will you let me play soccer with the boys?"

She turns to me. Her eyes grow wide. From somewhere inside her the old sparkle comes back to light up her face.

"Aunt Lena, will you?"

For the first time since we came to the barn I hear her laugh.

A soft laugh that no one else must hear.

SPRING RITES

What's that? Speak up, child, I can't hear you!" Uncle Teo is at his desk, tapping a pencil against his knuckles. He is annoyed with me. It's March, we've been back from the barn for two months, but still I whisper.

I try again. "Supper's ready." He makes a silly face to look like mine, I guess, mumbles something, then leans forward and shouts, "Supper's ready! Is that what you said? Say it so I can hear you!"

I cringe, cover my ears. He grabs my wrists and forces my hands down. "Go on, say it!"

I take a deep breath and scream, "Supper's ready!"

He nods. "That's better. Now I hear you."

I don't remember how long it took before my voice came back. After four months in the barn I jumped at the slightest noise. All talk sounded like shouting—I was always hushing everyone. Aunt Lena was patient. "We're back home, Katinka," she kept reminding me. "You don't have to whisper anymore. And stand up straight!"

I had trouble with that, too, worried that someone might see me.

Did my voice grow louder day by day? All of a sudden? I can't remember, but when it did, Uncle Teo was still not happy.

"With that child chirping all day long, a man can't think!"

He is annoyed—I can tell by the way he keeps hitting his knuckles.

"Open a book," he commands. "And if you must sing, sing outside, in the garden!"

I can't go out or read today—there is work to be done. Anka and I are getting ready for Easter, we're dyeing eggs and decorating them with Slovak designs. In her hands they become beautiful. In mine they break.

"Anka, please, help me. I want one egg that's more beautiful than all the others."

"Oh-ho!" she says. "For whom?"

For whom, she asks, as if she didn't know! For Pavel, of course. I loved him all I could, long before we had to hide in the barn, but now I love him more than ever. That place inside me where love comes from must have grown those long hours I waited to hear his whistle—one long, three short—our signal to lower the rope.

On the nights Pavel was to come, Uncle Teo would be as impatient as I was every day. Through cracks between the boards he'd watch the stars come out, and worry.

"He's never been this late."

"Nonsense," Aunt Lena would whisper. "He doesn't start out till dark and then it takes an hour."

Pavel would come once a week to bring us things we needed, news about the war, and money to give the Husárs for hiding us in their barn.

"Something must have happened, Lena, or he'd be here by now. Those exemption papers are a trap, revoked without a warning."

Dear Jesus, don't let anything happen to Pavel. Forget about everything else I keep asking for, just keep him safe and make him get here soon. *Please.*

Footsteps. I hold my breath. But they pass and no one whistles. Uncle Teo shines the flashlight on his watch and groans.

Whistling. But it's not Pavel's signal, it's a song. I know the words. "Just one more drink, my pigeon, and I'll be on my way . . ." Must be someone on his way home from the inn. Crash! "Ježiš Mária!" He kicks something, swears at it some more, then moves on.

We lie in the dark, the only sounds our breathing and Uncle Teo's restless thrashing in the hay.

Suddenly, voices. A man. A woman. They must have stopped just outside our barn. They're talking softly, but I catch some words. He is begging for a little kiss. She's saying no, no, no, and giggling. At any other time I'd want them to stay, to listen to them, but now they're keeping Pavel away. He might be close by, watching, waiting for them to leave. Silence. Are they kissing? I press my ear against the space between the boards but shrink back from the wind.

None of us hear his footsteps, but his soft whistle, when it sounds at last, is like a trumpet from heaven that starts my heart racing. Uncle Teo lowers the rope. To hide my excitement, I make believe I'm asleep.

Pavel climbs the rope to our alcove. I listen to the whispered greetings, to the usual questions: How was the walk—did anyone stop him, talk to him? Is his job still secure? Has anyone come to the house looking for us?

"No, they haven't," Pavel answers. "The deportations stopped. No one knows why."

"Maybe it's because there are so few of us left in Slovakia. It's not worth their while to run the trains or pay the Hlinka Guard to run the operation."

"It can't be because of money, Lena," Uncle Teo tells her. "The Hlinka Guard would gladly work for free to get rid of the last Jew."

"One still hears of Jews sent to work camps here, in Slovakia, but no train has left for Poland since late October. That's two months, Father. I think it's safe for you to come home." Home? I pinch myself to make sure I'm not dreaming. But then Uncle Teo says, "No deportations today doesn't mean there won't be any tomorrow. We're staying. What's new at the front? Have *they* advanced?" Pavel switches from Slovak to Hungarian so I won't understand. Does he suspect I am not asleep? But I do understand. *They* stands for the Russians, and I am not supposed to know that Uncle Teo and Aunt Lena want *them* to win the war.

When I hear him opening his knapsack, I sit up, rub my eyes, yawn.

"Greetings, little cousin. Did I wake you?"

"U-hmmmm!" I want to fling my arms around his neck, to kiss his face a thousand times, but instead I whine, "Yes, you did."

From under his blanket, Uncle Teo shines a flashlight on things coming out of the knapsack: bread, cheese, a sausage, crackers, a jar of honey, canned cherries. Clean underwear. Towels. For each of us, a book.

"Aunt Lena, look! *Gulliver's Travels*!"

"Shhhh! Quiet."

I should have gone while we were waiting. Why didn't I? Now I need to go so badly I can't wait another minute. I roll closer to Aunt Lena and whisper in her ear.

She sighs. "Let Pavel take you."

Pavel take me? What an idea!

"I'll go by myself."

"Katinka, it's all right. No one can see, it's dark."

I am afraid to go by myself. I let Pavel take me. We slide on our bellies through the tunnel and come out on the other side choking from the dust.

Pavel holds my head inside his jacket to muffle my coughing. I love the smell of his jacket, love having my face pressed against his stomach. I keep coughing after I don't need to.

He takes my hand. We tiptoe over the planks, five steps to the pail.

When we get there I panic. I can't, I won't do it in front of him. I'd rather die first. Or explode!

"Pavel, please . . . take me back."

He turns off the flashlight, walks away as far as he can, and stands with his back to me.

I squat over the pail. He can't see me in the dark. His back is turned. But he can hear. With all my will I hold back.

In the moonlight that seeps through the cracks of the barn walls I see Pavel's elbows lift, like wings. He is covering his ears. Plugging them shut.

At that moment I let go and along with the relief comes a feeling of love so strong that tears spring into my eyes.

"Pavel," I whisper to his back, to his shut ears, "I love you, love you, love you . . ."

"For whom, eh? For whom that egg more beautiful than all the others?"

"You can guess, Anka. You'll help me, won't you?"

She does. When she is done, it is by far the best-looking egg of all. I wrap it in an embroidered, lace-trimmed handkerchief and hide it in my dresser.

On Easter Sunday, Uncle Teo doesn't sit in his office at his desk. "A lost day," he grumbles. The shrieking and giggling start early in the morning.

The village "gentlemen" come to our house with perfume or cologne to sprinkle Aunt Lena. They chase her around the dining room table while she makes squeaky little noises, covers her face, ducks. Whenever Anka shows up, they squirt her, too. They only smile at me—Pavel's little cousin.

Aunt Lena offers colored eggs from a basket, serves drinks.

"To your health, gentlemen!"

"To yours, dear lady."

The pharmacist shows up. The doctor. Božena's father, Škvorka, comes in civilian clothes. The other policeman stays away. So does the manager of the sawmill. Aunt Lena worries. Are they going to fire Pavel, their only Jewish employee?

"He'll keep his job," Uncle Teo assures her. "They can't replace him, a bright engineer, while all the others are away in the army."

"The principal from Katinka's school, Rospačil, hasn't shown up either."

"He might yet."

"Nor has that louse Radko."

"He's running for mayor. He can't be rubbing shoulders with Jews."

"Last year the mayor himself came. With the judge."

"They came to meet you, to congratulate us. We had just married."

"I saw the veterinarian a few days ago. He tipped his hat, said he'd come to us today."

"That bastard turned Fascist. Joined the Hlinka Guard."

"They're all joining, Teo, from Bundig, the judge, to Andrej, the chimney sweep. It's frightening."

Aunt Lena glances at the nearly full basket of Easter eggs. Standing behind the curtain, she watches the road, but there are no other gentlemen headed for our house.

Pavel is home for the holiday. I spent days thinking which dress to wear today, but when he comes out of his room he doesn't so much as glance at me. Oh, Pavel, don't you see how much I have grown? He doesn't. He is in a hurry to get out, to sprinkle the village ladies. Bumps into me, doesn't even say "Excuse me." Squirts Aunt Lena and Anka with lilies of the valley but doesn't waste a drop of it on me.

The garden gate squeaks open. The village boys storm through like a herd of bullocks. They're looking for Anka. If they find her, they'll drag her to the river and empty pails of water over her. Or they might hold her under the pump.

"Where is she?" they ask me. "You know?"

I shake my head. They run past me, around me, in and out the garden gate, the toolhouse, the shed. They don't see Anka crouched behind the raspberry bushes. I am by the vegetable patch, in full view, but no one pays attention. I blink back my tears.

"Hey there! What makes you think *you* can stay dry?"

Zasran—Shithead—the village cowherd, is straddling the fence, the goatskin water bag he takes to the pasture swung across his shoulder. Who is he talking to, I wonder. Did he spot Anka?

"You, with the freckles. Just wait till I get ahold of you!"

Me? He means *me*? I can't tell where he's looking—he is cross-eyed—but there is no one else around. He must be thinking I am someone else, an older girl. When he gets closer he'll see his mistake. He'll walk away.

But he doesn't. He grabs me by the wrist and pulls the cork from his water bag with his teeth.

"No!" I shriek, wriggling myself free of his grip. "No!"

I run. Limping, he follows. I hear his loud breathing. "No, no," I scream for Anka to hear, behind the raspberry bushes. "No, no, no," I shout loud enough for Aunt Lena to hear, in the kitchen. But it's Pavel, most of all, I want to hear my screams. "Don't you dare," I shout the loudest I can. "Don't you dare get me wet!"

The panting behind me stops. What happened? Did Zasran tire? Change his mind? Did he slip and spill what was left in his water bag? From behind the shed I peek back. Zasran is stretched out under the nut tree watching the clouds.

"Did you hear?" I yell, darting out from behind the shed. "I said, don't you dare get me wet!"

He sits up, yawns. How lazy he is. No wonder the cows stray into the corn.

"You wouldn't dare, would you?" I taunt him, skipping around the nut tree.

He shrugs. I make myself trip and fall at his feet.

"Help! I'm hurt!"

He grunts, gets up, starts walking away. Oh, no! I can't let him take off. All that screaming and not one wet spot on me to show for it. There'll be no end to the teasing. "Katarína, you were squealing like a pig under the knife. Who were you running from, a ghost?"

"Come back," I whimper.

"What for?"

"Water. I need to drink. I'm going to faint."

He turns around and says, "I'll get some from the house."

"No! You've got some on you, haven't you?"

I pull myself up just enough to lean on my elbow. Kneeling, he holds the open goatskin bag to my mouth. He smells of cows and smoke and sweat. I grab his wrist and make the bag tilt. A stream of water pours down my blouse and into my lap.

"Help, help, you're drowning me! Stop!"

Zasran scrambles to his feet. Without one look back he scales the fence and disappears.

I rush out into the street.

"Look at me! Dripping wet, soaked to the bone."

Drenched and screaming, the older village girls run from the boys while the young ones, standing behind fences, watch.

Pavel, where are you? Look at me! I am not your "little cousin" anymore. I've been *dunked*!

There flies Poluška, maid of the village doctor, chased by the miller's son. Why does she bother running? She can't get any wetter. And Marka. A water nymph. Is it water or tears streaming down her face?

"Poor Marka, they got you. Me too! Look."

"Got *you*," she scoffs. "A likely story. The milk's still dripping from your chin."

Tonka and Terka, twins from my class, point at me,

sneering. "What did you do, Katarína, jump into the laundry tub?"

"I got dunked."

"Oh, sure. By who?"

If they knew, they'd never stop laughing.

"By *who*?"

"One of the big boys."

"You're a liar, Katarína."

They stick out their tongues at me. I make donkey ears at them.

There's a chilling wind. I shiver in my wet clothes, but I don't want them to dry. Not until Pavel sees me. I'd better hurry home. He might be back by now.

He isn't. I sit in the kitchen, listening for the garden gate to squeak. When at last it does, I jump to meet him, but it's Anka, whimpering, who waddles through the gate. Her golden hair clings to her cheeks, her thin embroidered blouse to her breasts. A trail of puddles follows her to her room.

My blouse is dry. My skirt, almost. The few wet spots shrink and fade under my eyes. Pavel, where are you?

I creep into the bathroom. Thumb over the nozzle, I open the faucet. It's not cheating—my clothes were wet before, I'm just keeping them that way.

Aunt Lena finds me. "Katarína, what are you doing? You'll catch a cold, you silly! Take that skirt off at once!"

She has me sit in the kitchen, by the fire. My skirt is drying on a hanger above the oven. It's getting dark. The birds are settling down in the nut tree.

The lump in my throat won't go away.

That beautiful Easter egg I was going to give Pavel is in my dresser, wrapped in a lace-trimmed handkerchief. I won't give it to him. I *won't*, even if he walks in this very minute and pours the whole bottle of lilies of the valley over me.

But he doesn't walk in. Not this minute, not the next. And when he comes home, what then? He'll pay no attention to me or the skirt drying over the oven. Or he might, only to say, "Hey, you clumsy, what happened? Spilled some milk over yourself?"

I saw more of Pavel when we were in the barn. The nights he came, we'd spend hours together, lying next to each other, whispering in the dark. We'd play our game of "Who'll catch whom watching," as we did the very last time he came.

"Still not asleep?" Pavel asks.

"I was."

"With open eyes?"

"They were closed."

"Not when I opened mine—I caught you watching me."

I pretend I am offended, shift noisily in the hay, turn my back to him. Will he let me sulk?

"You're shivering."

"I'm not."

"Come closer."

"No." But I wiggle backwards, close enough for him to grab me.

"Now I've got you!"

I squirm. Kick. Bite his hand.

"Are we friends?"

"We're not!"

"You want me to let you go?"

No, no, never! "I don't care."

Uncle Teo and Aunt Lena are asleep. If anyone is watching us, it's Igor the spider, or a mouse. Pavel tweaks my nose. We're friends again. I breathe in deep. His hands smell of green wood, of cigarettes and the brown paste he scrubs them with when he comes home from the sawmill.

"Poor Katinka," he whispers, "you must be very bored, it's been more than three months. But it'll be over soon, you're coming home."

"We are?" I've been asking to go every day, for weeks, but now I don't want to. I'd like to stay here, with Pavel, and never, never move. "When?"

"In a few days. Aunt Lena didn't want to tell you until it's sure."

"Is this your last overnight here?"

"I hope so."

I don't. At home it'll be like before. He won't see me, won't have time for me. Even this night, his last, will be short. He must leave while it's still dark to get back before dawn. Through cracks between the boards I watch the stars. I wish I had a million hands to make each of them stay up, to keep the dawn from coming.

Pavel is asleep. My lips are so close to his chin, they're almost touching it. Would he wake, I wonder, if—

"It's bedtime."

—if I very, very lightly—kissed it?

"Did you hear me?"

"What—uh, yes, Aunt Lena?"

"I said, it's bedtime. Your room is warm. Anka lit the fire."

"What time is it?"

No answer.

"What time is it, please?"

Aunt Lena is sitting at the kitchen table, looking at me. She shakes her head.

"What's wrong?"

"Katinka, we're not in the barn anymore. We are back home, remember?"

"I know we're home."

"Then why do you *whisper*?"

ONE DRIED SPIDER, THREE CAT WHISKERS

Tonight will be a full moon, the first since Whitsunday. Tonight I must do it.

It'll be a while before it gets dark: today is the longest day of the year. At supper I'm quiet, I can hardly eat. Aunt Lena feels my forehead. I smile, sprinkle some more ground walnuts on my noodles, and force down another spoonful. Aunt Lena mustn't worry. If she does, she'll come to my room at night and find an empty bed.

Tomorrow evening, Pavel comes home. My heart beats faster at the thought. At this time we'll all be sitting at the table and I will feel Pavel's eyes on my face. He'll be looking at me the way he sometimes looks at Anka, when he thinks no one's watching. No wonder. Anka is eighteen, with golden hair and rosy cheeks. On Sundays, when she puts on her embroidered Slovak costume, she's got everyone gaping at her. But tomorrow Pavel won't have eyes for Anka; he'll be looking at *me*.

I help Anka with the dinner dishes. My hands are

trembling. Another hour before Aunt Lena sends me to bed, then two more before I leave. How do I stay awake?

Raisins! I'll need them in case some imp tries to trick me. I'll take a pocketful. And Pavel's picture. At that I can gaze for hours, but one glance at Pavel himself makes my head spin. I want him to look at me. Then, when he does, I blush, stutter, run away, and hide. But tomorrow I won't hide. Tomorrow night, when Pavel looks at me, I will be beautiful.

It's getting dark. The birds are back for the night, chirping in the nut tree. At midnight the full moon will be overhead, and I know what I must do.

Aunt Lena sends me to the pantry for bread, cheese, and an apple, tomorrow's lunch for school. I find the raisins and rush to my room to hide them.

In my dresser, under a pile of woolen stockings, is the box. Inside it are all the things I need for tonight with the instructions on a folded piece of paper. How scared I was to go to that witch—it took me forever to work up the courage. But Saint Katarína wasn't answering my prayers and Old Krasovka has magic powers.

"Don't go empty-handed," Anka warned me. "Take a sausage and show it to her as soon as she opens the door."

Old Krasovka's hut stands at the edge of the forest. It looks as if it's about to cave in. Scraps of boards pieced together. No windows, no chimney. The day I set out to see her, I carried a sausage rolled in a sheet of newspaper. My teeth kept chattering all the way. I nearly turned back three times. When I got there, my hand was shaking so hard I couldn't get it to knock. Suddenly the door swung open. Old Krasovka's witch power must have told her I was there.

"Get away, you little snitch," she screeched. "You have no business here!"

I stood frozen to the spot. She was all in black, hunched over a walking stick. Mean, squinty eyes, hair growing out of her pointy chin, a long, bony nose. Old Krasovka was even uglier than I remembered.

She raised her stick and pointed it at me, like a magic wand.

"Away! Didn't you hear?"

No sound would pass through my throat. All I could do was shake off the newspaper and dangle the thin white sausage in front of her. She stared at it as if it were a dead snake. Then suddenly her face changed. Long, sharp teeth jutted from her mouth in what, I guess, was a smile. She pulled the sausage up to her nose, to sniff.

"Who are you, little sweetheart?" she cooed. "What do you want? Come in, come in."

The stench inside made me nauseous. I was afraid I'd retch.

It smelled of rotten meat, of moldy cheese, of mothballs and strange things with odors so sharp they brought tears to my eyes. The only light came from a round opening in the ceiling and a wood-burning stove that had a large, steaming pot bubbling on it. There were shelves with bottles and glass jars of all sizes. Some of them had things crawling inside. Dried weeds hung in bunches from the ceiling. Old Krasovka pointed to a broken rocking chair for me to sit on.

I shrieked. Something had swooped down, fluttered over my head, perched on my shoulder.

"Don't be scared, love, that's Žigmund. Just making friends with you."

Žigmund was a raven. Pus oozed from his right eye. Another bird limped around the table with a leg propped by a splint.

"They'll be out of here in no time." She chuckled. "Old Krasovka knows her business."

She promised to help me, too, but I had to come back a few more times, each time with a longer sausage, before she would tell me what to do. On my final visit she made me write down her instructions and read them back to her from beginning to end.

"Nonsense," she muttered when I told her I had already tried dipping my face into a bowl of pickle juice, dabbing it with yogurt, and patting it with rose petals soaked in dew. "Silly nonsense! You count fifty days from Easter, that's Whitsunday. Then, on the night of the first full moon, you do everything exactly as I said. You can look in the mirror only in the morning—"

"The morning! You mean I have to wait till—"

"Be quiet and listen! After the cock crows twice, but before he crows for the third time, then, *only* then must you look. Do not fall asleep," she warned me.

"But what if—"

"No *ifs*, Katarína, this is magic! If you look too soon or too late, you'll undo it!"

"All right, all right, I'll wait . . ."

. . .

Aunt Lena calls me back into the kitchen. At nine o'clock she kisses me good night and sends me to bed.

I slip the nightgown over my dress. In the mirror I see a gawky fourth-grader with red hair and freckles. I hate the freckles, hate them! It's because of my freckles Pavel keeps looking at Anka, not at me. And in school it's "Freckleface, Freckleface, what's that all over your face?" "She fell asleep under the apple tree—the sparrows got her!" "Nah, those are bat droppings!" "Fly spots!" "Spiders' eggs!"

The mouth twitches, the chin trembles. The mirror ripples, blurs. I wait for her to appear. She is beautiful in her green velvet gown and soft, broad-brimmed hat. Clear skin, rose-colored cheeks, a slender waist. She is I, in only a few more years. "Don't go," I plead, even as Freckleface, with red eyes and a shiny nose, pouts back at me. I stick out my tongue at her. "I won't see *you* again," I tell her. "Good riddance!"

I am not allowed to read in bed after nine-thirty but I do, under the covers, with a flashlight. *Grimm's Fairy Tales.* I read them over and over again. In my favorite stories I am the princess in trouble and Pavel is the prince who rescues me. Every prince has Pavel's face; every princess has the face I want to have.

My nose hits the page. Ouch! I've been dozing. I jump out of bed, check the clock. Another hour and fifteen minutes to wait.

I try reading some more but can't keep my mind on it.

I keep glancing at the clock and I worry: Will the garden
gate squeak and wake Aunt Lena? Will someone from
the village see me? Is everything I need in the box? I
take it out of the dresser and check each item against my
list: one dried spider, three cat whiskers, a clove of garlic,
the tail of a mouse, droppings of a bat, and the ointment
Old Krasovka gave me. For the umpteenth time I read
the instructions. It's past ten o'clock. I close my eyes and
think of Pavel.

I fell in love with Pavel the moment I saw him, last
year, in April, when Aunt Lena and I came to live in
Uncle Teo's house. Pavel and his father came down the
gravel path to meet us. "Light as a feather," he said, lifting me so high that my hair tangled with a branch of the
nut tree. "Kiss Pavel," Aunt Lena prodded, "he's family.
Your new cousin." He was looking up at me, smiling, and
I felt heat coloring my face and rushing down my neck.
"Put me down," I shouted, wrenching off a fistful of ten-
der new leaves. "Down, down!" "Look at her blushing,"
Aunt Lena said, laughing. There I was, up high, for everyone to see. "It's not true." I burst into tears. "I'm not b-b-
blushing!" Pavel lowered me gently and covered my
cheeks with his palms. Smells of cigarettes and something else—like the rosin I used to rub on my violin bow
or the yellow sap I scrape off trees. It was then I felt it for
the first time. I didn't know what it was but knew I
couldn't stand feeling any more of it. I grabbed Pavel's
hand, bit it, and ran.

Pavel's hands smell of machine grease even after he

scrubs them with the brown paste. He comes home only on weekends, and sometimes, on Sundays, he'll hide a chocolate bar under my pillow. I love chocolate. There isn't much of it around anymore, and when I get some I gulp it down in one minute, wishing there were more. But the bar Pavel leaves me lasts almost a week. I mark five even sections on the wrapper, and every evening after I brush my teeth I eat one fifth. That way, the less chocolate there is left, the happier I am.

Sunday nights I force down my first bite. The chocolate clogs my throat like soggy cotton—Pavel will be gone at sunrise. If I'm lucky, I wake to the bounce of his bike on the steps or to the squeaking of the garden gate. From behind the curtain I watch him adjust his knapsack, tuck his pants legs into his boots, mount the bike, and ride down the hill. I stay at the window long after he disappears behind the poplar grove.

Mondays, tulips are pale, lilacs have no scent, sunflowers droop. Books are boring, games aren't any fun. After school I climb to my perch, high in the nut tree, and don't come down until dark. At night I take my second bite of Pavel's chocolate. There's still such a big piece left of it, I could cry!

Tuesdays, I begin to think about the past weekend. I see Pavel everywhere: sketching at his desk, oiling his bike in the hall, blowing smoke rings across the kitchen table. I think about the times he looked at me, about what he said, what I answered, and what I wish I had answered. I don't talk much to Pavel, except in my mind.

Across the kitchen table I'd be telling him—in my mind—"I love you, I missed you so much." But when he breaks into my thoughts with "Got all your homework done?" I only nod or grunt.

In the evening, on Tuesdays, the chocolate tastes good, and after the third bite there's less than half of it left. I begin to wonder what to wear to dinner on Friday.

Wednesdays, I daydream. I tiptoe into Pavel's room and hug his pillow. I sniff his sweaters, his Sunday jacket, his belts, cigarettes, matchboxes. In the bathroom I rub the soft bristles of his shaving brush over my face, open the jar of brown paste he scrubs his hands with, unscrew the tube with the goo he rubs into his hair to make it smooth and shiny. The scents bring him so close I can feel his breath on my cheek. I am grownup, beautiful without the freckles. Arm in arm we walk along the river, watch the sunset, whisper secrets to each other . . .

Blackbirds, thrushes, robins, swallows—where did they all come from? On Thursday mornings, long before Anka wakes me, I lie in bed listening to them. From the kitchen come smells of roasting grain for our make-believe coffee and the cakes Aunt Lena is baking for the weekend. On Thursdays I can jump over the brook where it's the widest, make the stones I throw skip in the river. In class, I score the highest grades and laugh when my classmates call me Freckleface. The last piece of chocolate tastes the best. Slowly, I roll it in my mouth, crush it with my tongue, feel it melt. Was it I who a few days ago wished there were none left?

Fridays are impossible. I spill my milk, tear my shoelaces, break pencil points, stain notebooks with ink. Rocks trip me, walls bruise my nose, doors slam on my fingers. Every few minutes I rush to the mirror to try out another hairdo, hold yet another dress up to my chin. But in the evening, when I'm asked to set the table, I do not set a place for Pavel.

"Another plate," Aunt Lena reminds me. "It's Friday."

"Is it?" I ask. "Are you sure? The week went by so fast!"

Anka giggles. Aunt Lena smiles. "Put on a pretty dress," she tells me.

"Oh, must I?"

"Well, if it's too much trouble . . ."

But I'm already at the door, eager to break into a run on the other side of it, impatient to make myself beautiful.

Beautiful for Pavel! What time is it?

Nearly eleven! Off goes the nightgown. I trace garlic around my lips and over my belly. Krasovka's ointment goes on my wrists. One cat whisker inside my sock, it doesn't matter which. Shoes must be worn the wrong way: right shoe on left foot. Pockets! This dress doesn't have any—I'll wear the one with the ruffle. A clove of garlic and the ointment go in one pocket, the instructions and Pavel's picture in the other. The raisins! Here, with the garlic. The rest of the things stay inside the box. I tie a kerchief around it to make a bundle and leave.

Quietly, I turn the lock. The garden gate squeaks, but no light appears in the window, no one calls after me. Do

I take the back way, behind the barns? No, it'll rouse the
dogs. The tavern's long been closed, no one's coming
home at this hour. The night watchman, cross-eyed
Fučík—I must watch out for him! A few gulps of
slivovitz—plum brandy—and he sees the Devil everywhere! If he spots my shadow, he'll scream and take to
his heels—I'll have the whole village after me! "Katarína,
what are you doing out at this hour?" "Where are you
going?" "What's inside that box?" I can't tell the truth.
Old Krasovka said if I did, she'd turn me into a frog.
Brrrr! A mushy, slimy frog, squatting on a rock. Puffing
my cheeks, croaking. A muddy pond for a home, flies for
dinner. Webbed feet and those horrid eyes that pop and
swivel! I'll never tell the truth, not if they torture me!
Ouch! My shoes are torturing me; I should have practiced wearing them the wrong way. I'll never make it!
No, I *will*. I'm almost at the cemetery; that shadow is the
edge of the forest.

I'm hot from walking fast and cold from being scared.
My knees are shaking. What's there? Something's moving above that mound—holy saints, a ghost! That's a new
grave; the spirit's hovering over the corpse. Dear Jesus,
I'm afraid. Aunt Lena, help! What am I doing here, in the
middle of the night? I'm going home. Let Pavel make
eyes at Anka, I don't care! Here is his picture, in my
pocket. Let me look at it, tell him, to his face, "Pavel, I
don't care if you make eyes at . . ." Oh, he's so handsome!
I love you, Pavel, love you! I *am* going to the forest.
Tonight is full moon, the first since Whitsunday; tonight

is my chance. Krasovka's ointment will keep me from harm; she said it would and I believe her. It stinks enough to drive off a million ghosts!

Can I run? It hurts, but I do: down one hill and up another, stopping to catch my breath only when I reach the forest. I've never been in the forest at night. At night and *alone*. My teeth are chattering. The instruction sheet trembles in my hand. I hold it up to the moon and read: "Enter forest, take first turn right, follow path to Saint Anton's shrine . . ." A steep climb. I rest at the shrine, then look for a moonbeam between the pine branches. "Circle shrine three times. Continue walking. When path divides, turn right." I know that path: it goes to the Virgin's shrine. It's not far, not more than—

"Help! Help!" Something's clutching the ruffle of my dress. Claws are digging into my thighs and ripping the backs of my knees!

"Let me go!" I lurch forward, stagger to the nearest tree, wrap myself around it. With my cheek pressed against the bark, I listen to my breath—it's loud enough to wake a bear! Who grabbed me, I wonder—the Devil? "Phew, phew, phew!" I make the sign of the cross. "May the earth swallow you!" Is he following me? I listen. No sound of hooves or smell of fire. Slowly I turn my head. There—something's moving over the bramble bush. I take a step closer. A strip of cloth, caught on thorns, flutters in the breeze. My hand slides down the side of my dress to reach the ruffle and touches bare skin. Rats! What do I tell Aunt Lena?

In the shrine I kneel down to pray: "Blessed Mother, stop my teeth from chattering or they'll break—I'll look like an old, toothless *baba*. Forgive me for stealing that last sausage for Krasovka, I had no money left! And the walnuts, too, I needed them to trade for the mouse's tail. Please don't let Aunt Lena find out, and keep her out of my room tonight. I'll never lie or steal again, I promise. Here, I'm leaving you most of my raisins. I may need the rest to keep imps from playing tricks on me . . ."

I walk to the fallen oak and find the rock with three crosses painted on it. This is the tree that fell on the woodsman, and the rock marks the spot where they found his body. His ghost haunts the woods, Krasovka said, but I was not to worry, her ointment would protect me. I am to grind a clove of garlic into the rock, then jump backwards over the fallen oak. I bet some imp is lurking about, waiting for me to trip, so he can get at the raisins. May they color his teeth purple!

This part of the forest is too dense to roam in; few people do. It's dark even in daytime. I shiver. There are smells of mildew, of moldy mushrooms and rotting wood. I trip over roots, tangle in knotgrass, step into puddles ankle-deep. The path disappears. I inch forward, push one branch from my eyes while another claws at my throat. Twigs hook into my hair and pull at my bundle. My whole body itches as insects scurry down my back and my nose twitches in a coil of spider's yarn. Is this the path, I wonder, or a snare? Have I strayed into forbidden grounds with no way to turn back?

Suddenly, the forest opens. Before me is a wide, moonlit clearing, and at the far end of it gleams the Witches' Pool. There I must wait for the first stroke of midnight and do what I've been told.

I cross the clearing and crouch among the weeds. What a stench! Do witches bathe in this water, I wonder. Do they drink from it? I open the bundle and drop in the box. It disappears, comes back again, and rests on the surface of the pool.

Black clouds rush past the moon, which has turned silver and risen high in the sky. There's a cool wind—my skin feels bumpy with goose pimples. I wedge my chin between my knees and wrap my arms about them. Hoot! Hoot! My heart skips a beat as I glimpse slits of green light in the laurel. I gasp. Something leaps in the grass. It's a frog. "Hey, frog, tell me, were you a little girl once? Did Krasovka punish you for not keeping a secret?" That won't happen to me, I won't even think about it. I'll count to one hundred: that will pass the time. One, two . . . I wonder what time it is? Three, four . . . That tree has eyes and a mouth. An evil mouth. Five, six . . . Those long, spiky branches want to grab me! Seven, eight, nine, ten, eleven . . . Something's moving in that bush! Twelve—there, again! Thir—what's that sound? Someone's breathing behind my back! Holy Katarína, save me! There—it stopped. Thirteen, fourteen, fifteen, sixteen . . . That cloud is like a huge head. The head of an ogre. Seventeen, eighteen, nineteen . . . And there's a flock of black sheep trying to escape from him. Nine—

where was I, nineteen? Yes. Nineteen, twenty, twenty-one . . . The box is still floating. Why, I wonder. Don't the witches want my gift?

BONG! BONG! The church bell! It's midnight! In a flash I'm on my knees, bending over the Witches' Pool. I cup my hands, dip them into the . . . the . . . is this *water*? It's thick like porridge and it stinks! I retch as I force it to my face. No, I can't do it! My fingers open and globs of dark mush drip back into the pool. Weeds, sleazy with slime, cling to my hands. BONG! BONG! I'm running out of time! I must do it. Do it now! I pinch my nose shut and with my free hand splash—no, smear the stuff over my face. "Bagic powers of de dight, geep by vre . . ." I gasp for air. No, this won't do, I can't hold my nose shut. I'll try again, that time won't count. "Magic powers of the night"—splash—"keep my freckles out of sight!" Splash, smear. "Magic powers of the night"—smear—"keep my freckles out of sight!" Splash, splash. "Magic powers of the night . . ."

The echo of the last bell still hums as I lie stretched out in the weeds, panting. My face itches with little things crawling over it, but I can't wipe it: old Krasovka told me not to. I must hold it to the moon to dry and then the thing is done.

Done!

The thing is done, my freckles are gone! They're gone, *gone*! I can't look until dawn, till after the cock crows twice, but I know they're gone, I can feel it!

"They're gone!" I shout, leaping across the clearing,

my arms outstretched, like wings. "My freckles are gone,
I am beautiful!"

Pale clouds move across the sky, but there's no howling ogre and the trees don't have arms that want to seize
me. Something's moving in that bush—a bird, or a field
mouse rushing home—and those green lights in the laurel are the eyes of an owl. It's past midnight. It's Friday.
Tonight . . .

"Hey there, owl," I yell, my hands cupped around my
mouth, "tonight Pavel comes home! Hey there," I shout
loud enough for anyone in the forest to hear, "tonight
Pavel will fall in love with me!"

I twirl, skip, slide down the path. I pat the rock with
the three painted crosses, hop over the fallen oak. The
Virgin in her shrine is smiling at me. I blow her a kiss,
then race up the hill, past the cemetery, and through the
village streets, to our house.

"I am beautiful, beautiful," I shout to the Whitsun
moon as I throw open the garden gate, fling my arms
around the nut tree, and swirl round and round . . .

PARTING

O ld Krasovka, you horrid witch! May all the sausages you eat turn into turds and grow out of your nose!"

Those were my words when I saw my face in the mirror. Freckles, freckles, not a single one missing. And that scarecrow blamed me!

"You must have done something wrong, Katarína," she said, "or the magic would have worked."

"I did what you told me to," I shouted. "Everything. Exactly."

"You fell asleep before the cock crowed for the third time, did you not? That undid the magic. The freckles came back . . ."

I bet they never left. All her magic did was to get Anka and me in trouble. My cries woke up Aunt Lena. She saw my ripped dress, my muddy shoes, the muck and slime on my face. I was punished for going to the forest at night; Anka was told to pack her bags for giving me the idea. She cried, said she never thought I'd do it. Aunt

Lena forgave Anka. It took a while before she forgave me.

I look in the mirror and feel a surge of anger, same as that morning, three months ago. Ugly, ugly. Tomorrow Zorka is coming to take me to Mariška Plčková's house. Will the Plčko children make fun of my freckles, too?

Zorka, who brings us butter once a week from Klietky, is in the kitchen talking with Aunt Lena.

My bundle is prepared—I'm ready to leave. I am not only ready, I am impatient, because today I will be sitting in the coachman's seat, holding the reins. I will command the horse, making it turn left or right, making it stop or go. Zorka promised me that last week, when I cried. Since then I haven't cried. I have thought only of our ride to Zorka's village, Klietky. I have even practiced in the shed, astride the chopping block, cracking an imaginary whip over an imaginary horse: *"Dio! Che-hee! Hejtah! Prrrrrr!"*

Aunt Lena's eyes are red this morning. She is pale.

Last week she told Zorka she was going to the county hospital for an operation and after that for a few days' rest in the mountains with Uncle Teo. She didn't want to leave me with Uncle Teo while she was in the hospital, she said. He was busy, away from the house much of the time, and didn't have patience for a nine-year-old. She was afraid I would be lonely, and was looking for a family to take me in. Ten days, two weeks at the most, at twenty crowns a day, paid in advance. And the child wasn't much trouble, Aunt Lena added. She could be left to play by herself for hours and wasn't fussy about food. Would Zorka be willing to take her to her home?

"I can't, ma'am. I was going to tell you. We're leaving for Germany, the whole family. My brother and I will be working in a munitions factory."

Aunt Lena sighed.

"The pay's very good. Many young folks are leaving."

"I'm sorry we won't be seeing you anymore, Zorka. And sorry that Katarína can't stay with you. She needs a temporary home. Do you know of another family who might take her in?"

"Ma'am," Zorka said, "there's no home in my village fit for gentlefolk."

"Katinka feels good on a farm. Our Anka often takes her when she goes home for the day."

"But she is used to fine things."

"She'd rather be barefooted, climbing trees."

"Children on our farms don't have books or toys."

"That doesn't matter. She'll bring her own."

"As you please, ma'am. I'll ask Mariška."

"Mariška?"

"Mariška Plčková. She won't be going to Germany: her mother died, she is raising nine younger brothers and sisters. Katarína wouldn't be lonely . . ."

Aunt Lena is right. I am always happy to go with Anka to her parents' farm. I like climbing the apple trees in Dodák's orchard, racing barefooted across Radko's pasture—if the bull isn't there—playing hide-and-seek with my classmates in and around the Sledkos' shed. I would much rather stay at the pond with Tonka, minding geese, or help Terka cut grass, than do homework in my room. But when it starts getting dark I run home. I want to have supper with Aunt Lena, and at bedtime I want her to tuck me in with a good-night kiss. Two weeks is a long time. Two weeks away from Aunt Lena . . .

It was then my chin started to tremble. I flung my arms around her waist and cried.

"Poor little one," Zorka said. I felt her pat my head. "Don't worry, doctors are smart, they'll fix your aunt up perfect."

I wasn't worried about an operation; my aunt had lied to Zorka. She and Uncle Teo were going on a trip to get false papers so we could move to Hungary. They weren't deporting Jews there, and Uncle Teo worried that they might start again in Slovakia.

"Aren't you ashamed, Katinka?" Aunt Lena asked, stroking my hair. "I just told Zorka that you are a big girl, easy to take care of, and here you are, crying like a baby . . ." Her voice sounded as if she, too, was about to cry.

"I tell you what," Zorka said. "If Mariška Plčková says you can stay with her, I'll come for you with my brother Karol, in the cart. You can sit in the coachman's seat and hold the reins and crack the whip. Would you like that?"

Would I like that? There was nothing in the world I would have liked better! My last tear was still tickling my chin but I was already smiling brightly at Zorka.

Aunt Lena is handing Zorka an envelope fat with money and a note for Mariška Plčková. The note, my aunt told me, says that I am not her niece but an adopted Christian orphan. I am very happy about the *Christian*. I've not been wearing the Star of David, as Jews are supposed to, and now I won't need to worry about getting punished for breaking the law.

Zorka's eyes open wide. "So much money! What if I lose it?"

"It'll be safe. I'll pin it inside Katarína's coat. And where is Karol, why didn't he come in?"

"Oh, no! He's in his work clothes, not fit to—"

"Nonsense, Zorka. He should have come in, had a drop of slivovitz, for the road. Now, Katinka, are you ready?"

"Yes. Just one more thing I left in my room."

Not one thing, two—the picture cards of saints and the rosary—those I couldn't give Aunt Lena to pack. I'll be carrying them in my pocket.

She did pack the books I wanted: *Gulliver's Travels, The Prince and the Pauper, Little Lord Fauntleroy.* Zorka said the children in her village didn't have any books. They'll like these, my favorites.

I'm also taking dominoes and playing cards called Sloppy Peter, games I'll teach the Plčko children. And, of course, my monkey puppet, Stefie.

On a shelf in the parlor is a photo album. Quickly, I leaf through it, pull out a picture of Aunt Lena, and add it to the saints and the rosary in my pocket.

"Can we go soon?"

My aunt is filling a tin box with cookies she baked for the Plčko children.

"Yes. Put on your winter coat."

It's much too warm for a winter coat, but I obey. I am impatient to get to the cart and climb onto the coachman's seat.

Aunt Lena pins the money envelope inside my coat and picks up my bundle. Yesterday I saw her stuff some of my winter woolens in it. She is absentminded. It's September and I am leaving for two weeks at the most, I won't be needing them.

We walk down the steps into the garden and stop outside the green, latticed gate.

"Be good, Katinka. Don't annoy Zorka with too many questions!"

"I'm going ahead, ma'am. Let me take the bundle and get her seat ready."

"Thank you, Zorka."

A breeze rustles the chestnut tree. Something drops between the branches and plops on the ground.

"Aunt Lena, look, a chestnut. They're starting to fall!"

She nods.

"In two weeks, when we're all back, will you help me thread some into a necklace?"

She nods again.

"Promise?"

She pulls me to her, roughly. Her woolen dressing gown makes my nose itch but I don't pull away. I like Aunt Lena's smell. I only turn my head to take a breath.

The lilac bushes around the gate are still wet with dew.

I feel Aunt Lena trembling. She holds me so close I think she will crush me, and suddenly I feel afraid. Her sobs send a chill through my belly.

"Ready?"

A gruff voice. Must be Karol.

"Yes, she is coming."

Aunt Lena pulls a handkerchief from her pocket and wipes her tears. She always turns away when she cries, but now she is looking into my eyes, hers swollen and red. I see her lips move but can't hear what she is saying, her palms are pressed against my ears. I think she said, "Bless you!"

The horse neighs. I can't wait to get hold of the reins.

"You're making such a fuss, Aunt Lena. I'm leaving for only a short time."

She spins me around, pats my backside. "Go, Katinka. Go."

I run. Zorka helps me up. Karol, seated on the coachman's box, grunts a greeting.

"When we get out on the open road he will let you take the reins."

I don't argue with Zorka. I can't very well tell her that all week, in my imagination, I have been riding through the village holding the reins in full view of my neighbors and classmates.

Karol cracks the whip. The cart jolts; we're on our way. I look back and wave to Aunt Lena; then we turn a corner and I lose her. The horse strains up the curving road. Each time it snorts, a puff of vapor rises and circles the tips of its ears. There once again, now below us, is the chestnut tree and, partly hidden by it, our gray house with its red-tiled roof. Inside the green gate, under the lilac bushes, stands Aunt Lena, waving goodbye. She and the house disappear at one bend, then reappear at the next, smaller. When we get to the firehouse, I'll be allowed to take over the reins. That scrawny horse! Can't it go any faster?

We are passing the last of the run-down huts near the top of the hill. At the firehouse, Karol pulls over to the side of the road and halts.

From here we can see all of the village: the brook with its many wooden bridges, the church, my school, the fountain in the village square. I follow the road from Janík's tavern to the house of Tomáš, the baker, and from there to the large chestnut tree through which I get my last glimpse of our red-tiled roof. I shield my eyes the better to see, but there doesn't seem to be anyone standing inside the gate.

"Here's where you take over the reins, Katarína."

I don't move. I am gripped by fear, the same I felt in Aunt Lena's embrace. "Two weeks," I tell myself, "only two weeks!" But I begin to wonder: Has Aunt Lena lied to me as well?

Aunt Lena lied to Zorka, and, in her note, to Mariška. Those winter woolens in my bundle—did she *mean* to put them there? Winter was two months away! Is that why she was crying? Was she saying goodbye to me for . . . for . . .

"No, no, no!"

"Hey, where are you going? Stop her, Karol!"

Karol grabs my wrist and pulls me back to my seat.

"Don't worry, Katarína, your aunt will be well again. The time will pass quickly!"

My knees are shaking. I whimper but cannot cry. I want to tell Zorka that Aunt Lena lied to her, to Mariška, to me. I want her to get angry and take me back.

"Karol, let her have the reins!"

Karol slips the reins between my fingers, then winds them around my wrist. "Give a good shake and shout *dio*!" he orders.

My hands tremble and my throat is choked with tears. I cannot shout the command.

"Let's go, or I'll take the reins! I haven't got all day!"

"Easy, easy," whispers Zorka.

She lied to me. Aunt Lena is a liar. I hate her.

I grip the reins firmly. My hands stop trembling. I don't want to see her again—she tricked me. I don't want to see her again, ever!

I am not whimpering anymore. I feel strong. I hate Aunt Lena, hate her!

"*Dio!*" I shout, shaking the reins. "*Dio!*"

We lunge forward.

The horse races down the hill and still I spur it on.

The cemetery, the little chapel, the old mill. Saint Štefan's shrine. Old Krasovka's hut. I want to get away, far from Aunt Lena, and never come back!

"*Dio!*" I shout above the clatter of the wheels.

"*Dio, dio!*" I howl against the wind.

KATARÍNA WAITS

From the hilltop behind the smithy I watch the road to the village. I climb the hill a few times a day. I am waiting for Aunt Lena.

Now that the poplars have shed their leaves I can see even farther down the road, but I can't look for long. The sharp October wind brings tears to my eyes and whips the fringes of my shawl against my face. Inside the smithy it's warm. I can hear them working. I would like to watch, but the blacksmith won't let me. He says I could be blinded by sparks.

Someone is coming down the road. A woman. She is too short to be Aunt Lena. It's that gossipy Topka, I think, but Aunt Lena might still get here today. Maybe this afternoon.

"Hey, Kubo," I hear the blacksmith calling his apprentice. "Bring out the slivovitz for the shepherds."

Today the sheep are coming back from the mountains for the winter. From the hilltop I can see them bouncing down the mountain path. The shepherds have long, colored ribbons pinned to their hats and are playing on wooden flutes, but you can hardly hear the music for all the bleating and barking. Mariška Plčková is waiting for her family's three ewes—she cleaned the sheepfold yesterday.

"Hey, Kubo! Tell my wife to get some coins out from where she keeps them. The fatter the sheep, the bigger the tip!"

If I didn't love Pavel so much, I'd marry a shepherd. We'd roam the woods and meadows all summer long, then stay under a *perina*, a huge eiderdown, through the winter. But would a shepherd have me—a girl with red hair and freckles?

The sheep come home when it starts to snow in the mountains. I'll soon be needing the woolen things Aunt Lena packed in my bundle. What's keeping her, where is she? Are Uncle Teo and she packing, getting ready for Hungary? Would we be moving before Christmas? No, we'll celebrate Christmas in our gray stone house. How I miss it! Sometimes I make believe I am back home, perched in the nut tree, counting the chipped red tiles on the roof . . .

"One, two, three, four, five . . ."

The blacksmith is trying to count his sheep as they mill around, bleating. Under the big oak a lamb suckles, its thin little legs quivering with excitement. I want to pick it up and hold it, run my fingers through its fleece.

The blacksmith sees me coming. "Get 'em inside,

Kubo," he shouts, "out of harm's way. Hurry, damn it!"

"Brrrrr, brrrrrr," Kubo calls to the sheep as he kicks and shoves them into the sheepfold.

"Get in there, dumb beasts! And you"—the blacksmith turns to me—"stay away!"

His hand traces a sign to ward off the evil eye.

Mariška Plčková won't let me help her because, she says, I come from gentlefolk and work would spoil my hands. Poor Mariška! Her mother dead, her father a drunkard, and she, not yet twenty, raising nine brothers and sisters by herself. Whatever food from the farm she can sell she takes to the market—we never get to eat anything other than potatoes with buttermilk. The money Aunt Lena sent is long gone, but here I am, eating their potatoes, drinking their buttermilk, and there is never enough of either.

Not much longer, though. I'll be back home in time for us to choose a tree, bake cookies, and wrap candy to hang on the branches. Aunt Lena said we'd have a Christmas tree this year because of Anka, but she knows how happy it will make me, too. When she and Uncle Teo get back, they'll give the Plčkos all the money they owe for the time I've stayed here. That will be enough to buy a sheepskin vest for Mariška, warm stockings for Anežka, a reader for Milka. Miško will get the tall boots he is always eyeing, Ferko a harmonica, Vladko the tools he needs for work. For the twins, Ludo and Ludka, colored pencils and notebooks, for Danka a doll, and for little Ján we'll bring bags full of sweets from the fair.

It will be the happiest Christmas for everyone. How many more days to go?

"I like the ornaments you make, Milka. Would you teach me?"

Milka Plčková is ten years old, a year older than I. With her thin arms she pulls buckets of water from the well and carries them inside the house.

When Milka sweeps the earthen kitchen floor, she sprinkles it first to keep down the dust. I watch the droplets of water turn into designs, Slovak ornaments, the kind peasant women embroider on their Sunday dress. Milka makes them everywhere she can. After churning butter she'll pat it into an oval shape, then carve a design on it with the edge of a wooden spoon. When it comes out to her liking, she wraps the butter in cabbage leaves and takes it to the market or the parsonage to sell.

"Would you teach me, Milka?"

She shrugs and turns away from me.

All the Plčko children do that when I talk to them. When I try talking to other children in the village, they run away or are called inside the house by their mothers or older sisters.

I wish my hair were brown, like Milka's. I'd wear it in a braid, as she does, with a ribbon at the tip every day, not only on Sundays.

.   .   .

The flowers in our garden must be withered by now and the nut tree bare of leaves. It wouldn't hide me were Aunt Lena to call me to dry the dishes or to tidy my room.

Oh, if only Aunt Lena called me now, how I would run to her! I'd scrub, wash, dry all the dishes in the world if I could be in our kitchen watching her bend over the pots on the stove, tasting, mixing, shaking her head, nodding. When I get back, I'll always keep my room neat— books and games on the shelf, crayons and pencils in a shoe box, the rocks and pebbles from the river in pickle jars. No one will trip on my slipper, sandal, or shoe ever again. I'll fold my scarves, pick up my handkerchiefs, pair my socks, hang my ironed dresses in the closet. Some might not fit me anymore.

Why aren't Aunt Lena and Uncle Teo back? Has something happened to them? Don't they care that I'm here all alone, waiting?

"Up the river Hron, down the river Hron, the rainbow dips, drinking from its waters . . ."

It is Sunday afternoon. Kubo is leaning against the big oak, playing on his accordion. I leave my lookout post on the hill and run toward the music.

Some of the village girls, in embroidered blouses and vests, have joined hands in a circle and are dancing.

"No one can match the Slovak people in spirit, courage, or valor," they sing in their high-pitched voices.

I know the words of the song. I know the steps of the dance. Open the circle, let me in.

"Hey, Milka, Františka, Ruženka, Zuzka," one of the dancers calls to her friends. "Come and join us!"

A tight grin stretches across my face. My ears strain for the sound of my name.

"Up the river Hron, down the river Hron, the rainbow dips, drinking from its waters . . ."

I come closer. The circle tightens.

I often think I see Aunt Lena and Uncle Teo coming down the road and run to meet them. I run till I get close enough to see it's not them.

Yesterday I was sure I saw Aunt Lena coming to the village. A woman her height, carrying a suitcase and dressed in city clothes, was walking between the poplar trees. I leaped, ran, tumbled down the slope. Closer and closer I came, and still she looked like Aunt Lena till, standing in front of her, I looked up and saw the face of a stranger.

"Stop staring at me, little girl," she scolded. "Go away!" I stood there panting, not taking my eyes off her face.

"Phew, phew, phew!" the woman mouthed into her sleeve. She did that because of my red hair, to shoo away evil spirits. Then she crossed herself and continued walking.

I, too, started walking. I walked back to the Plčkos' farm but held back from crying until I got to the stable, to Svetlana. Svetlana has soft, large brown eyes. She has a good smell and her breath is warm. I sat on the milking stool, my nose pressed against her flank, and cried until the steady swell of her breathing rocked me to sleep. When I woke up I felt good. I rushed back to the hilltop to watch the road.

"Did you hear? Now it's the miller's cow!"

Across the brook, boys are cutting grass to take home in burlap bags. Bent low over their sickles, they move slowly up the pasture side by side, gossiping. They cannot see me crouched behind the weeping willow.

"The fourth cow to croak since she's come," says Martin, the blacksmith's son.

"They say Strelík's horse rears when she crosses the road!"

"It's true! Topka's nanny goat jumps on the chimney each time she passes their house."

"Zobák's cart overturned the other day. There wasn't a stone in sight. He says she put the hex on him!"

"She did. Grandma Zobáková swears to it!"

I feel goose bumps crawling up my arms but want to find out more.

Martin sees me step out from behind my willow curtain. His mouth drops open. His shaky finger points at me.

The grass cutters freeze in their stooped positions—only their eyes follow Martin's finger.

"Hey, boys, what are you talking about?"

My voice breaks the spell. They drop their sickles and bags and race to the village.

. . .

Mariška Plčková doesn't want me going to church with her. She says she doesn't like people staring and asking her questions. It's enough, she says, if I pray in the house.

Every day after supper, I kneel with the Plčkos at the feet of the carved Madonna for evening prayers. I stay in the kitchen, kneeling, after everyone else goes to bed because I pray for Aunt Lena to come back. Also, I don't like going to bed. The room I sleep in is cold and I am all alone. On the other side of the kitchen is the warm room, where Mariška sleeps. She, little Ján, and her four sisters in one bed, her father and four brothers in the other. Their beds are boards laid over barrels, with no mattresses, only sheepskins and hay, but with all of them snuggled against one another it must feel soft and warm. I often plead with Mariška to let me get in with them, but no, she wouldn't hear of it! I am a paying guest, she says, I must sleep by myself, in a proper bed. It is the big bed in which her mother died. I curl up under the bulky down comforter and, until I fall asleep, I talk to my puppet monkey, Stefie. I also talk to the Blessed Mother and to the Infant Jesus. In the picture above the bed he looks younger than little Ján, and he is sitting in his mother's lap.

I wish that I, too, could sit in the lap of our Holy Mother. She has a sad, narrow face, like Aunt Lena's when we were hiding in the barn.

"I saw you at the fair, Mariška, all dressed up in your Sunday—ah-ah-choo!—skirt."

Tonight the village women have come to the Plčkos' to help prepare feathers for stuffing. They sit on the earthen kitchen floor around a growing pile of down and take turns sneezing. Mariška has bagfuls saved as dowries for her sisters, even though she doesn't think any of them will marry. They are too poor, she says.

I have been sent to the cold room, to bed, but through a crack in the door I can watch the women work and listen to the gossip. Their fingers move quickly, stripping barbs off the shafts, fluffing the feathers. Tufts of down float all over the kitchen—it's like the snow in the glass paperweight Uncle Teo keeps on his desk.

Zofka, the midwife, winks. "Talking to Kubo, she was, our—ah-ah-choo!—our Mariška."

Mariška's cheeks turn red. She must be in love with Kubo.

Strelík's wife thinks the shoemaker's apprentice is courting a girl from the neighboring village. "A good match," she says.

"He deserves better," says Topka. "I heard a few things. Do you know that she . . ." The circle of flowered kerchiefs shrinks, the voices are too hushed for me to hear.

Tinka Zobáková tells stories about a red-haired Gypsy, a witch, in her sister's village. Topka hears moans coming down her chimney at midnight. The miller's wife sees little devils leaping out of burlap bags. "Speaking of devils," says Strelík's wife, "Grandpa Strelík saw some in the woods, the night he took the shortcut home from the fair."

"Folks see strange things after one drink too many."

"May have been partisans he saw."

"They had horns and long black tails. He swears to it."

"Devil, partisan, same thing," says Topka. "One wants to harm our souls, the other our country."

"Some folks think different. They say partisans want to save our country."

"From whom, Zofka?"

"The Germans."

"What's that? We're lucky to have them for friends. They're good to us. Look what happened to Poland, France, Holland, Belgium—"

"Topka is right. No bread lines in Slovakia, no one bombing us."

"But it's them started this war—"

"Shut up, Zofka. And tell those folks that think different they're talking treason."

"God have mercy on us. Where my cousin lives, partisans are raiding farms, breaking into storage rooms."

"In my sister's village they kidnapped two children. Keep your young ones inside after dark."

"They should only kidnap that strange child our Mariška's keeping. Did you hear how the girl frightened Father Chrupák's sister?" asks Tinka Zobáková. "The one visiting for Christmas. She says the child jumped out at her on the road and wouldn't stop staring at her."

"The way she keeps standing on that hill," says the blacksmith's wife, "I say she'll grow roots in it!"

"What's she doing up there, I wonder?"

"You're not the only one to wonder, Grandma Zobáková. There's been lots of trouble in this village of late!"

"My husband says she is no ordinary child."

"There's plenty shows that!"

"I wouldn't keep such a strange child in my house," says Topka. "Not for all the money in the world."

The others nod. "Show us that note the aunt sent, Mariška. Read it again."

Mariška goes to the cupboard and brings Aunt Lena's note. The women look up, but their fingers keep moving, adding down to the white mountain growing at their feet.

" 'I am going to the county hospital for an operation and am looking for a family willing to board our little girl. She is a Christian orphan we adopted when her parents died in a snow avalanche seven years ago . . .' "

Mariška cannot read. She has the note memorized from all the times she had the priest, Father Chrupák, and Velká Huba, the town crier, read it to her.

" '. . . I was told you were a respectable family in need of some extra income. Pinned inside the child's coat you will find an envelope with payment of twenty crowns a day for two weeks in advance . . .' "

"Twenty crowns!" exclaims Strelík's wife. "Not bad for—"

"Let her finish. Go on, Mariška."

" 'I expect to be back in ten days, two weeks at the most, but should the Lord will otherwise we will pay double for each additional day Katarína stays with you—' "

"Holy saints, Mariška, you'll be rich. That's three months the girl's been here."

"Not rich, Grandma Zobáková, but we badly need the money. There's so many of us to feed."

"Surely you don't need one more. Get rid of her, Mariška."

"But the woman might still come, Topka. Katarína is sure the couple she calls her aunt and uncle are taking her home for Christmas."

"Looks to me like the aunt died in that hospital."

"Hah! That's if you believe she ever went to one."

She didn't. Aunt Lena and Uncle Teo went on a trip. I found out the afternoon I came home early from school and walked into their bedroom. The curtains were drawn shut, the desk drawers open. Scattered all over the floor were papers, photographs, clothes. There wasn't an empty spot to step in. When my aunt and uncle saw me, they froze like statues. Uncle Teo was the first to recover. He shouted at me to go to my room.

After a while Aunt Lena came in, sat on my bed. "Katinka, I was going to tell you—Uncle Teo and I are leaving for a few days—"

"I know. You're going to get false papers so we can move to Hungary."

Her breath stopped short.

"Katarína, how do you know that?"

Oh, no! I had blurted out my secret. There was nothing to do but confess that I understood *much* more Hungarian than she thought I did.

"When did you learn? Where?"

"In Bratislava, from Ilonka and Irenka. From the maids we had. From you and Uncle Teo talking."

She shook her head, rolled her eyes. "All this time you understood us and pretended not to?" I thought she would scold me but her voice stayed gentle. "Well, little monkey, I have a secret to confess, too. I know about your night visits with Anka."

"You do? Who told you—did she?"

"No. One night I saw your bed was empty. I was about to knock on Anka's door when I heard your voice. You were reciting a passage from the catechism."

"But you didn't come in."

"Something stopped me. I went back to the bedroom and told Uncle Teo."

"Was he angry? What did he say?"

"He said, 'Anka is teaching the child something very useful.' He gave her a raise."

We started laughing, neither of us able to stop, the way we used to, sometimes, before Aunt Lena married. When she could talk again, she said, "We won't be gone long, ten days, two weeks at the most, and during that time you'll be staying on a farm—"

"With Anka's parents?"

"No, with people who don't know much about you or us. It's safer that way. We'll tell them you are a Catholic orphan we adopted. You won't have trouble with that, will you? You learned your lessons well."

Aunt Lena kept talking. She said that after the war she'll be the one to stay up with me nights, she'll teach me about religion. *Our* religion. She should have done that all along, she said, she was wrong not to. What the Rabbi said that time was true: all I knew about being Jewish was to be ashamed, that's why I wouldn't wear the Star of David . . .

I stopped listening. I was thinking about ducklings, kittens, chirping yellow chicks, about riding on top of an oxcart loaded with fresh-cut grass, about playing hide-and-seek among haystacks with new friends, same as on Anka's farm, only this time it would be for ten days, not one. Ten whole days on a farm . . .

"Get rid of her, Mariška, she's trouble."

Yes, Mariška, do what Topka wants you to. Take me home!

But if Aunt Lena and Uncle Teo aren't back yet, what then? Maybe they couldn't get the false papers where they went and had to go somewhere else. Or they're in a work camp. The blacksmith was telling Kubo there was a small, new one, close by. Surely they'd get time off for Christmas.

I kneel to say my prayers. In moonlight, our Holy Mother in the picture looks even more like Aunt Lena. I climb on the bed and kiss the folds of her robe. I kiss the chubby arms of the Infant Jesus in her lap.

You couldn't forget it's getting close to Christmas with all those sows squealing, running from the knife. I pull my scarf tightly over my ears and still I hear them.

Wagons and carts are under burlap, in sheds, and the

KATARÍNA WAITS ↔ 115

sleighs are out. They slide by so silently you can't hear one coming but for the bells on the horse's harness.

It takes a long time now to climb the hill. The snow is ankle-deep on the trail, and when I stray I sink up to my knees. Everything around is white—you couldn't tell there was a rabbit two feet away were it not for the pattern of paw prints in the snow. Our garden, too, must be all white, with only frost flowers climbing up the windows of the house.

Mariška's father brought back a pine tree yesterday— a small, scrawny one. Mariška says they don't have much to hang on it and even less to put under it. "There'll be lots of presents," I told her. "This Christmas there'll be presents for everyone." I am giving Aunt Lena a rosary. She might be upset, but only at first. I'll teach her to love Jesus and the Blessed Mother, and then every night the two of us can kneel and say our Hail Marys together . . .

"Father Chrupák, please, I'd like to ask something."

I've been hiding in the dark, behind the vestry door, waiting for him to come for evening prayers.

"Who is there?"

"It's me, Katarína. I'm staying at the Plčkos', Father."

"What do you want?"

"I'm nine years old. I'd like to prepare for First Communion."

"How come you haven't made your First Communion yet?"

I don't answer.

"Are you Catholic?"

"I believe in the Holy Trinity, the Virgin Mary, the—"

"I need to see your certificate of baptism."

"I don't have one. Here, I mean."

"I need authorization."

"Please, Father, I've been wanting to for so long—"

"Write for permission to your guardian. Can you write?"

"Yes."

"I'll write for you, to the county hospital. That's where she is, isn't she?"

I stare at my boots.

"Is she there?"

I clasp my hands behind my back to stop them from shaking.

"Answer me, child—yes or no?"

"Yes," I shout. "Yes!"

Yes—yes—yes. Echoes pound my ears, follow me down the aisle, out the door. I run without stopping, race up the cemetery road, fall on my knees at the shrine of our Saviour.

"Jesus, I lied. I lied to a priest."

I look up at our Saviour hanging from the cross. The agony he suffered for our sins. My sins. I hate Aunt Lena for making me lie.

"Lamb of God, I love you so much."

Blood sprouts along the rim of his crown and trickles down his temples.

"I lied to a priest, Jesus, inside a church."

A crown of thorns. Nails hammered through hands, through feet. How terribly that must hurt.

Now there are two roads to the village, the one I am watching from the hill, and the river, which is frozen solid. It's not slippery to walk on the river or drive over it with horses because layers of snow cover the ice. It's slippery only in places the children have cleared, for sliding. They stand in line and take turns on the long, narrow strips. I, too, would like a turn but can't get close—the children pelt me with snowballs. They pack them hard and aim for my face.

Only a few more days till Christmas. Through the smithy window I can see a tree all lit up and covered with angels' hair, the branches buckling under all the candy hanging from it.

Uncle Teo and Aunt Lena must have gone home first, to get things ready. I know I get in the way when my aunt is baking.

They could come on either of the roads—the one I'm watching or the frozen river.

I can't see the river road from the hill. Maybe, while I am waiting for them here, they've already come and are at the Plčkos', waiting for me.

I slide down the hill and race to the farm.

Last night I woke to sounds in the kitchen. I heard the door open, then footsteps and whispers. Mariška was crying. Or was I dreaming? That's what Mariška says, but then, why is she looking at me in such a strange way this morning and why are her eyes so red?

Through the crack in the door I saw the blacksmith and Topka. I couldn't hear what she was saying to Mariška but caught some of what the blacksmith said: ". . . must have been them . . . Topka's son-in-law . . . yes, it's sure . . . false papers . . . trouble for all of us." Even his whisper is loud.

Mariška said something and Topka hissed, "No, tomorrow! First thing tomorrow morning!" That's when Mariška started to cry.

The blacksmith said, "All right, two more days won't matter. No one else knows, do they? Keep your mouth shut, Topka."

Topka forgot to whisper. She said, "The day after Christmas. Promise, Mariška."

I pressed my ear against the keyhole.

I heard Mariška whisper, "I promise."

Mariška doesn't let me out of the house. All day yesterday I waited for Aunt Lena's knock on the door till, after supper, the Plčkos left for evening Mass. I begged Mariška to let me go with them, but she wouldn't allow it. I followed in secret on the footpath behind the barns, my kerchief pulled deep down over my forehead.

In church I couldn't sit still, I kept thinking about Aunt Lena. I saw her pacing the Plčkos' yard, calling me, wondering where I was. In the middle of prayers I slid off the pew and ran to the house so fast I couldn't stop panting till long after I got back and saw there was no one waiting.

My things are packed in a bundle, I'm ready to leave. Uncle Teo and Aunt Lena are also getting ready to leave, they are coming for me the minute everything gets done. I can see Anka trying to find space in the pantry for yet another tray of cookies, I see Uncle Teo bringing in armloads of firewood, enough to warm every room through the night.

Poor Aunt Lena can't stop to rest. Her cheeks are flushed from standing by the oven, from rushing so.

Tomorrow is Christmas Eve.

Tonight is Christmas Eve.

Mariška wants me to stay inside; she says my aunt and uncle can find their way to the farm, I mustn't stand on that windy hill all day. It wouldn't be all day, I told her. They'll be here early, in time for us to get home before dark!

Anka won't come with them; she'll wait for us at home. With her fingernail she'll scrape clear a spot among the frost flowers on the window to watch for our sleigh.

I bet her hands are trembling with excitement, like mine. I am going to the stable to hug Svetlana, then out to say goodbye to Kubo, Zofka, Grandma Zobáková, the Strelíks—I'd better hurry or I'll never make it back before they get here!

. . .

It is past midnight. They didn't come.

Mariška kept muttering, "I knew it, I knew it," but I know why they didn't come. I told her what happened:

Aunt Lena and Uncle Teo started out early but turned back because they forgot something—the money they owe Mariška, or one of the presents—and when they were about to leave for the second time, the weather changed. It did, this afternoon, didn't Mariška remember? The sky turned a yellow-gray and hung low, the way it does before a snowstorm.

They couldn't make the trip in a storm, could they? It was sad for them, too. No one touched the Christmas dinner or opened presents or stayed up to hear the church bells ring at midnight.

They went to bed early, to get an early start.

They'll be here tomorrow, Christmas Day, before breakfast. We'll have the rest of the day to celebrate. And all the days after that.

There are no sounds coming from the smithy; it's Christmas Day. The sun is slipping behind the mountains. Shadows grow long. The road stretches white and empty between the poplar trees.

TOWN CRIER

What's that, a drum? Must be Velká Huba—Big Mouth—with some official proclamation. But why today? He only comes Fridays. Mariška said I was not to leave the house, but if Velká Huba is back today the proclamation must be very important. I have to find out.

A shortcut—the footpath behind the barns. It's bumpy and slippery, with snow piled high on both sides. I hurry to get to the general store. It's the second stop on his route.

Where is he? What's taking him so long? The town crier is educated—he reads and writes—and for a glass of slivovitz he'll follow any farmer home to help with a letter or a note. That's why by his third stop he slurs words so badly no one understands what he is saying, and by the fourth he is likely to sing bawdy songs and forget all about the news. The times he doesn't make it to the end of his route he is stretched out somewhere, snoring under a tree or in someone's barn.

Tom, tom, trom-ti-tom! Here he comes. I can tell by the way he walks that he's had a few. The children trailing after him are not interested in the announcements— they want to listen to the drum and touch the shiny brass buttons on his uniform. Velká Huba wants everyone to see him. Short and bowlegged, he climbs the three steps of the store, throws out his chest, and keeps drumming.

All around, doors open, windows fill with faces. Bundled in sheepskin jackets and shawls, the peasants scurry down the footpaths between the wooden fences.

Tom, tom, tomtomtomtrrrrrrrrrr.

The drumsticks are moving so rapidly they turn into a fuzzy arc. Then, as the last stragglers join the crowd, Velká Huba gives three strong beats, and all sound stops.

"A-hem!" He clears his throat, then spits into the snow. Everyone watches as he gropes inside his vest for the scroll. Not the scroll, his flask! Slowly he unscrews it, takes a gulp, screws it shut, shoves it inside his vest. He is about to say something, but changes his mind. Takes out his flask again, swivels it. Another gulp. Another swivel.

"Hey, Huba! Get on with it!"

"Upon my word! Who's that? Strelík? Is a fellow not to warm his bones or moisten a dry throat? It's not me sits by a warm stove all day!"

"The news, Huba!" shouts Kubo. "What's so important that couldn't wait till Friday? Let's hear!"

The flask disappears inside his vest. He pulls out a

scroll, unrolls and holds it as far as his short arms will stretch. A few people shove their way forward.

" 'Mmmmmmmay it be brought to the attention of the general public,' " he reads, " 'on this day of the Lord mumble mumble, that all land taxes are to be paid by the end of this month. Whosoever fails to do so will be—' "

"Hey, Huba! For this you brought us out into the cold? That's old news! You read it last Friday!"

"Eh—last Friday? Yes, old news. Wrong scroll. Wanted to make sure folks are listening."

"Making fools of us, Huba. As if we had nothing better to do!"

"Just wanted to make sure everyone's awake. Daydreaming by the stove these long winter months, folks get drowsy!"

Sighs. Giggles. Grumbling. Velká Huba takes out another scroll, squints at it, nods, and starts to read:

" 'Mmmmmmmay it be brought to the attention of the general public on this day of the Lord, January mumble mumble, that partisans have been sighted in the forest north of the old mill. Partisans—' "

"Holy saints! When—"

"Quiet! Go on, Huba."

" 'Partisans are servants of the Devil. Anyone helping them is helping the enemy. In time of war this is treason for which the penalty is death by firing squad.

" 'Should anyone have any knowledge regarding partisan activity or know of persons sympathetic to their cause and fail to report such information, they, too, will be considered guilty of treason and subject to death by firing squad.' " Velká Huba turns his head, looks at the frightened faces around him. Satisfied, he rolls up the scroll, takes off his hat, and bows.

"On behalf of the County Council I bid you a good day."

For a few moments the crowd stays silent, then the shouting starts, all at once.

"May the Blessed Virgin protect us!" "That vermin is upon us!" "May those traitors roast in hell!"

I look for a familiar face. There, bundled in a black shawl, is one.

"Grandma Zobáková, who are partisans?"

She blinks at me with small, frightened eyes and walks away.

"Milka, are partisans really servants of the Devil?"

Milka Plčková purses her lips and follows the town crier to his next stop. I ask the blacksmith's wife, "Please, who are partisans?"

She rests her hands on her wide hips and squints at me. "They are your aunts and uncles. They've come to get you!"

The villagers standing nearby laugh.

"What did she ask?"

"She wants to know who partisans are."

"As if she didn't know!"

"I bet she's spying for them. Nothing but trouble in this village since she came!"

"A Gypsy, giving us the evil eye!"

"God is punishing us for Mariška Plčková's greed!"

"Listen to me," a woman shouts. "All of you, listen. I found out. I know the truth."

All eyes are on Topka. She has taken the place of Velká Huba on the steps and stands there, wheezing. "I know the truth about that girl. She's no Christian orphan. They lied to Mariška. Tricked her." Topka's hand clutches at her heart; she is gasping for breath. Her eyes are slits set deep above her pudgy, trembling cheeks. "She's a Christ killer," Topka shrieks, pointing at me. "A goddamn Christ killer!"

Faces are turning toward me. I want to run, but my knees are giving way. It's all I can do to stand up.

Strelík climbs the steps and stands beside Topka. "Jews are enemies of the Slovak people. We're sheltering an enemy. Let's get her out of this village, quick!"

Topka nods. "I kept telling Mariška, 'Get rid of that girl,' but she wouldn't listen."

"My husband was right. He kept saying all along she was no ordinary child."

"How did you find out, Topka?"

"That couple they caught, with the false papers. They were—"

"Those, two months ago?"

"Those."

"They were shot."

"Deported to Poland."

"No, sent to a labor camp here, in Slovakia."

"They're rotting in the county jail."

"Never mind *them*. How do you know the girl's not a Christian orphan, Topka?"

"My son-in-law found out. Looked up records. She is a Jew."

"Harness the horses, somebody, get her to Headquarters. What are we waiting for?"

"Grab hold of her, Strelik. Don't let her get away."

"Hurry. Who's ready to—"

A whistle, long and shrill, cuts through the voices. Kubo towers above the crowd.

"Hold it, all of you. Listen."

"No time for speeches, Kubo. We're in danger every minute she's here."

"I'm with you, neighbors, I don't want to get shot either. But let's not panic. Look at the sky—it's going to snow. Heavy. There's no way of getting her to Headquarters before it closes."

"We're wasting time. It never closes."

"The important persons won't be there. Do we hand her to the janitor? We must make sure she gets into the proper hands. Mariška and I will take her first thing tomorrow morning. I promise."

"*Promise!* I heard that before, Kubo. Mariška promised to take her right after Christmas. That was ten days ago."

"She meant to, Topka, but her father took sick and she's got nine little ones on her hands."

"I kept my mouth shut because she promised. We could have been shot."

"We didn't know how dangerous it was. Tomorrow morning, Topka, you have my word."

Strelík nods. "Early tomorrow is better. But be sure to emphasize to the right persons, Kubo, that Mariška was tricked—she was told the girl was a Christian orphan, the Plčkos needed money, that's how she came to be here."

"Right. And don't let on that anyone here knew ten days ago. Just say we did the right thing the minute we found out."

"All this trouble because of that evil little—"

A snowball crashes against my mouth. Pain strikes me like a whiplash. I bolt.

The road is icy. I keep stumbling and falling. Snowballs, hard as rock, slam against my back. I cover my head with my arms and stagger along until the snowballs no longer reach and the curses shouted after me break up in the wind.

Inside the Plčko stable, I bolt the gate and fasten the latch. Blood drips from my lip. Svetlana turns to watch me with soft, dreamy eyes. I drop onto the milking stool and howl into her flank.

HEADQUARTERS

G et up, Katarína. We have to leave soon."
It's still dark outside. Why is Mariška waking
me? Where are we going?

I duck under the covers. My stomach feels tight. I
know that I don't want to go even before I remember.
We're going to Headquarters. Topka and the others made
Mariška promise she'd do it.

While I dress, Mariška packs the things I'm taking into
a bundle. Stefie is hiding under the pillows. I stuff her
into my coat pocket. The rosary, too.

Sleigh bells. That's Kubo. Last night he told Mariška
he'd borrow a sleigh and the mare from the blacksmith
and take us. Mariška hands me a chunk of dark, sour
bread and a cup of buttermilk. "Here, drink it. We have
a ways to go."

In the other room, Milka is asleep with all her sisters
and little Ján in one bed. I wish I could get in with them.

It's cold. Kubo is putting a blanket over the mare. He's
wearing a sheepskin jacket and cap. He lifts me into the

seat, then helps Mariška. The wind blows through my coat. I'm glad when I am squeezed in tightly between Mariška and Kubo.

The mare shakes her head, impatient to leave. I look at the house and the yard one last time. I didn't get a chance to hug little Ján, to say goodbye to Mariška's father, to Milka or any of the others. When I come back after the war to get my things, I'll bring them lots of presents.

The mare's harness bells make a pretty sound. We glide silently over the frozen road. No one is talking.

I am remembering what people were saying yesterday: "Jews are the enemy of the Slovak people." "We'll get shot for sheltering the enemy." I love Slovakia, my country. I love Jesus. Why am I an enemy?

"Mariška, what will they do at Headquarters? Will they shoot me?"

"Of course not. Silly child. What an idea."

"What will they do, then?"

"I don't know. They might send you to a work camp. There's a new one close by."

"To do what?"

She shrugs.

Maybe I'll find Aunt Lena and Uncle Teo there. And my old friend, Malka. I close my eyes, lean on Mariška's shoulder, fall asleep. Next thing, I hear her talking.

"What will they do with her, Kubo?"

"There's no telling. But it's not for you to worry. You do what you have to."

"Why would they be sending a child to a work camp? What on earth can she do—sweep, dust, help out in the kitchen?"

"I hear bad things about the ones in Poland. Soldiers coming back from the front tell stories I don't believe."

What bad things, what stories? I want to ask but don't dare—they'd be angry that I'm awake, listening. Merciful Mother in heaven, watch over Aunt Lena and Uncle Teo. Don't let anything bad happen to them.

The sun is up, shining on my face, but it's still cold. I am shivering. There's no telling what happens at Headquarters, Kubo says. Headquarters is a monster that looms larger every minute, and I am riding straight into its jaws. In a fairy tale a handsome prince with Pavel's face would now be galloping to my rescue. I look at the white fields, at the frozen road ahead, but there is no Prince Pavel rushing to save me.

"Have you no faith, Katarína? Haven't you learned anything?" That's Anka's voice I'm hearing. "The only true prince is the Prince in heaven, Jesus. He loves you. And you have a patron saint watching over you. Pray to her."

I start praying to Saint Katarína, beg her to save me from Headquarters. I doze off again and wake up only when Mariška shouts, "Stop the mare, Kubo, I can't do it!" Her face is white and her hands are shaking. "Stop, Kubo, I mean it."

"Whoaaa!" Kubo reins in the mare. "Calm down, my pigeon," he tells her. "What's on your mind? We can't bring her back with us."

Mariška is crying. "She's just a child, Kubo. It's not right."

"There's lots that's not right. What are we to do?"

"Hide her. For the winter, at least. Maybe by spring the war will be over."

"Hide her where, in your house? You've only got those two rooms off the kitchen, and there's your father and the nine kids milling about."

"I don't know. The storage room, I guess."

"The kids will find out. They'll blab, get you in trouble."

"I keep the storage room locked."

"Your father'll kill you if he finds out. And I gave my word to Topka, promised her in front of everybody, we'll take her to Headquarters."

"I won't do it, Kubo. My heart tells me it's not right."

"You've got a soft heart, pigeon. Look, we're nearly there. Let's stop at the next inn, talk some more. If we bring her back, we'll have to stay awhile. Can't bring her back in daylight."

Mariška wipes her tears with the tip of her kerchief and nods. I want to hug her. Instead, I hold back my own tears and pray. "Saint Katarína, you made Mariška change her mind, you saved me from Headquarters. Dear Patron Saint, thank you, thank you a million times. But please, don't let Mariška get into trouble because of me. And one more thing. Do I have to be locked up in that icy storage room, all by myself? There are mice in there. Big fuzzy spiders. Rats. Help her think of some other way to save me. *Please.*"

STEFIE

You're up, Stefie? Did you sleep well? I didn't. Matilda kept me up. I mean, her babies did, with their squeaking. She moved them to a new hole, somewhere between the potato bin and the corn. Didn't you hear?

Guess what—I have to pee. Stefie, if a good fairy appeared now and said, "Katinka, you may make a wish, one only," do you know what I'd wish for? To not have to pee. Not ever again!

Listen: clicker-clacker, clicker-clacker, they're taking out the mare. The ground sounds hard, it must not have snowed last night. The harness bells! It must be Thursday; Mariška's going to the fair. Why the sad eyes, Stefie? She'll be back tonight, and before she leaves she'll come in to empty the pail and bring us buttermilk and bread. Hungry? You are! Well, I have a surprise. Close your eyes. Sniff. Yes, it's sausage, I saved a piece. We'll eat it slowly. Mariška says there's none left and there won't be any more till next Christmas. Here, have some. Open your mouth, Stefie, you've got food stains all over your face. How funny! I'd have them, too, after I'd pull my face out of the mixing bowl. Aunt Lena used to tease me about it, say, "Go to the bathroom, Katinka, look in the mirror." You could tell the kind of cake she was baking from the smudges on my face. If they were brown, it was chocolate; if yellow . . .

Stefie, you're crying! Why? I didn't mean to make fun of you—you're beautiful, even with sausage spots. Here, I'll kiss them, every one of them. This one, under your nose, that one, on your chin, and this one and that one, and that one!

I can't hold it anymore. Come with me, Stefie. Let's count to ten and then we'll roll out of these sheepskins, both of us. One, two . . . Look! It's so cold I can see my breath. N-o-o-o! I'm not getting out from under the covers. Let's forget about having to go. Try to sleep some more.

I bet Mariška would like to sleep some more this morning. She and Kubo were back last night. I wonder what they were doing on that heap of burlap bags. The noises they make! The sweet talk! My pigeon, he says. Oh, Kubo, she says. My dumpling, he says. Oh, Kubo, she says. Hey, Stefie, let's play a game. We'll pretend we're them! You speak in a low voice, you're Kubo, and I'll be Mariška. You start.

"Come to me, my pigeon, let me warm you."

"Not yet, Kubo, she's not asleep." Your turn.

"She is. Listen to her snoring."

"I'm worried, Kubo."

"About us? Why, she can't—" Oh, I forgot to change my—I mean, you must make your voice low, Stefie, like this: "About us? Don't worry. She can't squeal."

"It's her I'm worried about. Somebody'll find out."

"That's what I told you, remember? Any of the kids come in here?"

"No, but they used to. Now I keep it locked and they're wondering why."

"Just as I thought. But the war won't last much longer. It'll be over by spring, I bet."

"We have to find another place for her before then, Kubo."

"We have to find another place for you, Mariška. Right here, by me."

Giggle—giggle—giggle. Your turn.

"Closer, my dumpling. Let me feel you."

"Ouch!"

"Ah . . . that's better . . ."

"Oh, Kubo . . ."

Oh, Kubo, oh, Kubo, and then the noises start. It's too dark to see what they're doing, and besides, I have to keep my eyes closed, pretend I'm asleep. But Mariška's right. Remember, Stefie, how angry Milka was the other day? "Why can't I go in there?" she shouted at Mariška. "You take me for a Gypsy? You think I'll swipe a cabbage or a fistful of oats?"

I told Mariška it wouldn't matter if Milka did come in—no one can see me behind these bags, barrels, and bins—but she says they'd know someone is staying here from the way it smells. I guess it's the sheepskins. All those times they got soaked when I didn't make it to the pail.

Mariška says that we're to crawl to the pail during the day. She worries someone might see us now that the frost is melting off the window. She needn't. It's been a while since I walked, night or day. If it weren't for the exercises she makes me do, my legs would have turned to dough.

You know, Stefie, this was the first room I saw when I came to Klietky to stay with the Plčkos. Your eyes are growing wide; you want to know more. All right, I'll tell you, and then I'll go. Make *sure* I do, Stefie. Promise?

I don't remember much about the trip here. I fell asleep on the coachman's seat and woke up only when someone was saying, "Here we are, home." "Home?" I mumbled, blinking at the strange young peasant woman. I have never been in this cluttered yard or seen the log cabin with its steep, slanted roof. Then I remembered. The young woman must be Mariška Plčková and we're in Klietky, in the Plčkos' yard. I also remembered leaving Aunt Lena earlier that day and started crying. Mariška said, "Don't cry, Katarína, your aunt will get well, in two weeks you'll be back with her." But how could I believe that, Stefie? Aunt Lena lied to Zorka, lied in her note to Mariška. Had she meant two weeks she wouldn't have put winter clothes in my bundle. Aunt Lena lied to me, too.

Mariška took my hand. "Come on, let's wash that tearstained face before the others get home."

I followed her to a well. Around it was a stone wall that came up to my waist, and on top of it, tied to a rope, a bucket. Mariška lowered it into the well. I heard it strike water, then heard the water spilling over the bucket's rim as she hauled it up. "Cup your hands, Katarína." She dipped a tin mug into the bucket and started pouring.

"Ouch!" The icy water felt like fire on my palms. I looked at them. They were bright red, streaked with wide red welts.

"That's from holding the reins," Mariška told me. "You'll be all better by tomorrow." She moistened the edge of one of her petticoats in the mug and wiped my face.

Reins reminded me once more of the trip, of Aunt Lena, of home. My chin started twitching.

"What, crying again? And we just got that face all clean. You looked so nice."

The lump in my throat was choking me. I needed to be by myself somewhere, to cry.

"I have to . . . where is the . . . the . . ."

Mariška took me by the wrist and started walking. My eyes were too blurred with tears to see, but by the smell I knew we were passing the stable.

"There." Mariška pointed to an outhouse. "I'll be in the yard, feeding the sow."

I rushed in, pulled on a string to shut the door. What

a stench! I started to retch. There was no seat, only a round hole in the floorboards. I knelt, bent over it, and nearly dunked my face into a white heap of squirming maggots.

I bolted, did my crying outside. When the tears stopped, I went back into the yard. Mariška was there, walking toward the pigpen with a pail. I heard snorting and squealing but didn't see the sow. Nailed on the wall was a trough with a narrow, open space above it. The minute Mariška emptied the slop pail into the trough, the sow pushed her snout through that space and slurped her supper.

"A couple of weeks before Christmas we sell her," Mariška told me. "That's when pigs get slaughtered."

The poor sow, I thought, maybe that's why she's kept inside. It's easier to think about slaughtering if all one ever sees of her is a greedy snout.

This time it might have been the fate of the sow that started me whimpering. Mariška sighed. "Do you want to feed the chickens?" she asked. "I forgot to, this morning."

I don't think she forgot, Stefie. She wanted to take my mind off Aunt Lena.

We walked to the storage room. This room, Stefie. Mariška pulled a big key out of a slit pocket in her skirt and unlocked the door. A gush of chilly, musty air stopped me in the doorway. It was dark inside. After a while I could see bins, barrels, burlap bags along the walls and things I didn't recognize hanging from the ceiling, on hooks. I don't want to go in there, ever, I was thinking. I'd come out with spiders in my hair and mice chewing on my heels.

Mariška filled a battered pot with kernels of corn. "Call the chickens, Katarína."

"What are their names?" I asked.

She laughed. "They don't have names. Just call them, like this: *na pipky, na, pi, pi, pi, pi, na pipky, na . . .*"

I made my voice high, like hers, and suddenly—cackle, cackle, cackle! Chicken heads were popping out of everywhere, wings flapping, busy yellow feet rushing to me across the yard.

I started spinning while I tossed fistfuls of corn. The kernels dropped around me in golden circles. I imagined I was a captive princess and the chickens were bewitched knights come to my rescue. As soon as they made those golden circles disappear, I would find myself back in my kingdom and the chickens would turn into the handsome knights they were before. I kept tossing and they gobbled, gobbled, till there wasn't a kernel left, but nothing happened: there I was, far from home, and the chickens stayed chickens, cocking their heads, waiting for more.

Hey, Stefie—what was that? We heard the same sound yesterday. Mariška says it's the war coming closer, but to me it sounds as if the ice is breaking in the river. She isn't telling me, Stefie. She thinks I'd cry, that I'd want to go out, look for snowdrops, and go with the children to the river.

Remember what happens when the ice breaks, Stefie? The children drown the Winter Goddess, Morana. They throw her in the water and watch her toss and spin among the ice floes till she's torn to pieces. Then everybody joins hands and sings because when Morana is gone, spring is here!

Mariška is wrong; I don't want to go outside! I want to stay with you, Stefie, right here, under the sheepskins. I'm not afraid or lonely. Jesus is with me, and Saint Katarína's watching over us. I'll tell you a secret, Stefie. Will you keep it? May Saint Ján of Nepomuk help you.

Sometimes, at night, while you're asleep, the Holy Mother appears to me. You don't believe me. You think she'd never come to a place like this? You're right, I've never seen a holy picture of her in a storage room, but I swear, Stefie, I'm not making this up. When she's here I know it even before I see her. I get a feeling—goose bumps, shivers, but they're different from the kind I have when I'm cold. There's a soft sound, like the rustling of silk, maybe it's her robe, though she doesn't walk. She floats. I mean, she . . . what's that word? Milka kept saying it, the day she learned it in religion class—oh, I know! Levitate! She levitates, there, above the turnip bin, so close to me I can feel her breath on my cheek . . .

Look, Stefie, we have a visitor. Hi there, mouse, how's the family? You like your new home? I think Matilda's after our sausage. Do we give her some? Watch those whiskers wiggle! I guess we have to, she's our guest. Wheeee! Down the hole she goes! That sound scared her. Hey—that was the sound of an icicle crashing!

Quiet, listen . . . do you hear? Drip, drip, drip, all along the eaves. They're melting, Stefie! It *is* getting warm, though you'd never guess it in here—the water Mariška leaves us in the pitcher still freezes overnight. There—another one! And another.

Stefie, little one, do you know what that means? Kubo says the war will be over in the spring. And the roads will be clear. Aunt Lena and Uncle Teo can come get us. I'm not angry with Aunt Lena anymore. She didn't know it would take this long, she couldn't help it. Mariška says they must be hiding or they were sent to a work camp. Why that worried look, little one? The stories Kubo heard about camps, in Poland? Is that what you're thinking? What, then? Oh, Stefie! That's the silliest, craziest, stupidest idea you've ever had. No, they didn't go to Hungary without us. They'll be coming to take us home as soon as the roads clear. I promise.

Why are you sad? You don't want to leave Mariška? You're worried about Matilda? We'll be going back, to our house, our room. I bet you miss your friends there—is that why you're crying? I couldn't take them all. But I'm happy I took you.

Hey, sausage face, cheer up. We'll be waking up in our bed again, watching the birds in the nut tree, waiting for Aunt Lena to call us for breakfast, for Pavel to come home for the weekend. Beautiful Pavel. You know I love him, I told you often enough. Your ears are growing large, Stefie. You want me to tell you again what happened that first time I saw him?

It was in the garden. He lifted me so high my hair got tangled in the nut tree. Aunt Lena and Uncle Teo were laughing, watching me blush. I was shouting, "Put me down, put me down!" When he did, I was so angry I bit his hand. It was from then on that I . . . I . . .

Oh, Stefie! Ooooooh! Oooooh! Oh, no, how awful! I can't . . . it's too late . . . I didn't make it, Stefie! It's spreading under me, flowing down my leg. Hot. Burning. I knew it would happen, knew it. It's your fault. I told you to make me go, but you didn't. No, you must hear stories! Take that smirk off your face. You're not sad anymore, you're laughing. Get off my hand, you silly puppet! There—look at yourself. A glove with a monkey head—that's what you are, so don't you make fun of *me*!

Oh . . . the sheepskins are soaked. I feel them turning cold. Soon we'll be shivering, you and I, with nothing to warm us. Stefie. Sweet Stefie. Why did you let it happen?

You must be starving, Stefie. I am. I could eat a potato raw. Want me to get one? You're crinkling your nose. I know, we tried one before and couldn't get our teeth in. But that was in the winter. The potatoes were frozen then.

What do you think happened to Mariška? Is she sick? I bet there are people around, like the last time, and she can't sneak out. Hey, my stomach is rumbling, do you hear? Let's crawl over to the potato bin.

Someone's coming. It's Mariška. Cheer up, little one, you won't have to stay hungry all night. But now, quick, under the sheepskins you go. I bet Mariška thinks I'm too old to be talking to you.

"What took you so long, Mariška? We've been—I've been waiting for hours."

"I couldn't get out sooner. Here, Katarína, have some bread."

Mariška's voice sounds shaky. Has she been crying? She bends down to put the water pitcher next to me, on the floor. By the light of her lantern I see that her eye is half-shut and her cheek swollen.

"Mariška, what happened to you?"

"Eat. Then I'll tell you."

I tear a chunk off the dark, sour loaf; sneak some of it to Stefie. Mariška sits down on my straw pad. Her chin is trembling.

"What happened?"

"My father beat me. He says people are talking . . . saying I'm hiding you, or someone, here, in the storage room. He wanted to have a look. I didn't know what to do, I said I lost the key. That only made him madder. He said I'd better find it by tomorrow or he'll break the door down."

"You think he will?"

"Sure he will. But not tomorrow. He'll be leaving early to help set up stands at the county fair. From there he'll head for the tavern—he always does—spends what money he's made. Comes home drunk, yells, curses.

Drops down by the stove and snores through half the next day."

"And when he wakes up? Will he come in here?"

Mariška is crying again. I want to hug her, but she pushes me away.

"Katarína," she says in a voice that doesn't sound like hers, "you have to leave."

A lump of bread catches in my throat. I stare at her.

"*Leave?* To go where?"

She doesn't say anything.

"Mariška, but where can I go? Please . . ."

I stop myself. Sometimes, with Aunt Lena, I would plead, nag, promise this or that to make her change her mind. But Mariška can't. If her father finds out she's hiding me, he'll beat her. *Kill* her! That's what Kubo said the day they were taking me to Headquarters. "Your father'll kill you if he finds out . . ."

"When do I have to leave?"

"The day after tomorrow. Early."

A mouse scuttles past our feet. A granddaughter of Matilda's?

"What will you tell my aunt and uncle when they come to get me?"

"They won't be coming. Not before the war's over. Looks like they're in a work camp."

"Maybe they're back home, for a rest."

"Don't go looking for them in your village, Katarína. Folks there know who you are. They'll take you right to Headquarters."

Headquarters doesn't sound bad anymore. It sounds better than staying in the street or in the forest. Even berries wouldn't be ripe enough to eat, not for a long while. And there are partisans hiding out there. Servants of the Devil who kidnap children if they're out after dark.

"You'll leave most of your things here, just carry a small bundle. I'll scrub you clean and I'll let you have a skirt and vest that got too small for Milka. You wear them and no one will take any notice of you. There's plenty of orphans and Gypsy girls knocking on doors."

Aunt Lena used to give me coins to give to the Gypsy girls. But in some houses children pelted them with rocks and set the dogs on them.

"Mariška . . . I'm sorry your father beat you . . . does it hurt you very much?"

She starts crying again. I cry, too.

"It's a warm spring, Katarína. It's warmer outside than in here. Tomorrow I'll bake you a pigeon and bread to take along. And there's a few coins I saved up . . ."

I hug her. She lets me this time, hugs me back.

"I'd better get back to the house." She picks up her lantern, walks to the door. "Katarína—I'll pray for you."

You can come out, Stefie, Mariška left. You heard what she said, I can tell by that worried look on your face. Aunt Lena would get that look sometimes, remember? Hey, don't *you* start crying. None of that. We have our own patron saint and lots of other saints to look after us—Saint Hieronym, Saint Beňadik, Saint Mikuláš of Myra—they all love children. They'll help us. And there's Headquarters. It's not any monster. That's just a silly story you made up. Headquarters is a house. A house with rooms that are warm and safe. People are living in them. They won't harm us, Stefie, I promise . . .

SEVEN VOICES

YOUNG GIRL TENDING GEESE

I was the first to see her.

She was coming down the road with her bundle and crossed the meadow to where I was minding the geese. Funny-looking. Orange hair and brown spots all over her face. A flowered kerchief like they sell at the county fair, a soiled vest, a skirt of homespun cloth, but shoes the kind gentlefolk wear and that *silly* making-believe she was used to them!

She stopped at the pond to watch the geese. I knew she was watching me.

When she looked my way, I stuck out my tongue.

She grinned, moved closer. I raised my switch.

"Could you tell me, please," she said, ladylike, the silly! "Could you tell me—"

"Get going, beggar girl," I shouted at her. "Get going with your dirty bundle and your stinky lice!"

FIRST HOUSEWIFE

My husband wasn't home.

He was in the fields with the oxen, plowing.

It was early. I left the little one in the crib and went to the barn.

Something in the far corner caught my eye.

Under a pile of hay was a body. A small one. A child.

Oh-ho, I thought, caught ya! My eldest. Pretending he's going to school, but there he was, snoozing in the hay!

I crept up softly and was about to lay my hands on him when suddenly this creature leaps out of the pile!

It wasn't my child. Oh, no! It was a girl, and a frightful sight she was. Hair like fire and sores all over her face.

We screamed at the same time.

She was quick. By the time I came to my senses she had scuttled across the yard and was scaling the fence.

I didn't chase her. Not in my condition! I wondered: How did she get in? Why didn't the dog bark?

Near where we keep him chained I found leftovers of a baked pigeon. That little tramp had bribed our dog, may the earth swallow her!

MIDWIFE

I saw her in church.

I can't get to morning Mass now that the grandchildren are with me, so I go later, midmorning or afternoon. No one's there those hours. Sometimes I hear the sexton, muttering, going about his chores. It wasn't him I was hearing that day. It was a child's voice. I followed the sound till I saw her, a girl barely old enough to tend geese, kneeling at Saint Katarína's feet. She didn't see me; I was watching her from behind a pillar.

Who was she? I've been midwife to all the children born in this village, some of them grandparents by now, and there hasn't been one with that color hair that I can remember. This was no one's daughter, no one's grand-daughter. There was a dirty bundle beside her. Must be an orphan, I thought, so little and already on the road, on her own. The eyes of Jesus held me. The Sacred Heart, all kindness and love, was asking me to open my own. Take this little orphan, it was saying. Have mercy on the little one, she needs a home . . .

I was about to do it but, may the Lord forgive me, didn't. I'm not young, and it's all I can do to care for the four my daughter left, may her soul rest in peace. From what I saw of her face I could tell this child was sickly. She'd bring sickness into the house. "No, my Lord," I whispered, "I can't, have pity on me . . ." I said a prayer for the poor orphan and pledged a generous offering at Mass come Sunday.

SECOND HOUSEWIFE

She's not mute, the child. She talks when she wants to. And not shy. Cheeky, I'd say.

I was sitting on the stoop outside the kitchen, peeling potatoes for supper. Suddenly, there she was.

"Ma'am," she says, "I can help you with the potatoes. I can sweep the yard, churn butter, milk cows, fetch water from the well . . ."

I chuckled. "Can you? You don't look strong enough to lift a cup. Whose are you?"

I looked her over. A freckle-faced runt with a bundle. The embroidery on her blouse was the kind they do in Klietky, a two-day walk from here. Her sheepskin vest was worn and soiled, but her shoes . . .

"Hey, where did you get those shoes, steal them?"

She looked at me wide-eyed, then spun around in a huff, ready to take off.

"Pardon me." I laughed. "I didn't know I was talking to a lady."

A pity, I thought, watching her go, I could use help around here. Maybe she was stronger than she looked, and it wouldn't take much to feed her.

"Hey, come back," I called after her. "There's work to do!"

She came running. Put her bundle down, thanked me. Her eyes sparkled, and when they did she wasn't ugly. Still, I had my doubts. Her talk didn't sound like she was from here. Who was she? She had not answered my question. I asked again: "Whose are you?"

Her eyes darted from me to the road, her heel was twisting in the ground, but her mouth stayed shut.

"Lost your tongue?" I shouted. "Don't you hear? Whose are you?"

"God's," she snapped. Cheeky, wouldn't you say? Must be plenty she's ashamed of, that needs hiding. Those shoes. She's got fast fingers, that one, she'd take constant watching. It's not worth the bother. No, I decided, I'll not have a thief under my roof!

"If you can't talk," I told her, "pick up your bundle and go!"

She didn't move.

I handed her three potatoes from the basket.

"Here, bake them in the fields somewhere. Don't come near my house again."

Two of the potatoes she stuffed inside the bundle, one she kept in her hand.

As she walked down the road, I saw her rub it clean against her skirt, then take a bite and swallow it raw, with its peel, like an apple.

GERMAN SOLDIER

I stopped her. I wasn't even on duty that day.

Heinrich shouted, "Why bother with a child, Fritz?" But I did. On the contrary, the partisans might think it clever to send a little one with a bundleful of ammunition, but Fritz isn't stupid! I found out, on my last home leave, what war does to children. "Papa, do you know that the Messerschmidt Bf 109G has a 1,475-horsepower engine? Do you know that it flies 620 kilometers an hour? Papa, do you know that the Focke-Wulf . . . the Dornier . . . the Heinkel . . . the Stuka . . ."

I was learning the facts about our Luftwaffe from my son, a kid in kindergarten when I first left for the front.

It was hand grenades I suspected when I felt the hard, round shapes in the bundle the girl was carrying. They turned out to be two raw potatoes and the head of a monkey puppet. The monkey had a button in its ear: Steiff. Made in Berlin. As for the rest, there were two dresses, winter woolens, and such. The dresses were of fine fabric, stylish. The handkerchiefs were soft, mono-grammed, with crocheted borders. There was a Bible. Pictures of saints. A photo of a woman.

"Who is she?"

"My aunt."

I studied the face in the photograph. Light hair, intel-ligent eyes, a fine nose. A good-looking Aryan type. A bit too thin for me, but then, hmmm . . . perhaps not!

"Where is your aunt?"

"Oh, she's sick. Very sick. She's in the county hospital. I'm on my way to stay with cousins."

"The fancy dresses in your bundle—where did you get them?"

"Hand-me-downs," she said. "My aunt works for gen-tlefolk."

"Show me your papers!"

She didn't have any, but then, most of the villagers don't. When questioned, they just stand there with va-cant eyes, rocking on their feet, reeking of cheap slivovitz.

"You're lying!" I shouted.

She didn't wince. Kept muttering, fingering her rosary. I let her go.

But I called her back.

Something about the girl made me ill at ease. Her speech: not the local dialect. Not a peasant, but trying to pass for one. Why? And why was she carrying those two raw potatoes? They were not practical to eat on a trip, and they were laughable as presents for her cousins, even with the food shortage. Were they hollow? Stuffed with something? With what? Explosives? A coded message? Diamonds? Cyanide?

I untied the bundle, split the potatoes open with my thumb, and crushed them.

She picked the mangled pieces out of the mud.

I examined her belongings again, piece by piece.

When I was holding the puppet in my hand, the idea struck me: there was a message tucked inside that monkey head. The girl was a courier for the partisans. Making a monkey out of me! Furious, I tore open the puppet and ripped off its head.

She screamed. Then, with clenched fists, she threw herself at me. Me, an armed German, in uniform! I could have had her arrested on the spot, but in my mind I was already hearing the barracks jokes. "Did you hear? Fritz was attacked by a little girl!" "Show us your wounds, Fritz, are they healing?" "Fritz, you'll get a medal from the Führer for your brave stand . . ." *Ja, ja.* I know our boys! I let the girl rage.

There was nothing inside the monkey head. I threw it and the tattered glove into the gutter.

She leaped after them and clutched them to her chest, howling.

I've heard plenty of howling these past years but couldn't stand hers. She sounded like our dog after the car hit her. I had to shoot that bitch to end her agony and mine. The devil take it, if this one won't stop—

"Shut up," I shouted. "I order you!"

Not normal, this child. The same age as my son, I'd say, and still so attached to a toy. I guess war does that to children.

"Stop the noise," I commanded. "Your monkey is only a piece of cloth with sawdust stuffing. Give it to me!"

I had to pry it loose from her. Sniveling, she trotted after me to the barracks.

I hardly believe it myself, but so it was: his first free afternoon in two weeks Private Fritz spent sitting on his bunk with needle and thread, mending a puppet.

I did a good job, too.

When at last I finished, I held it up for her to see.

"Look, like new. Perfect. No one can tell a thing."

I've never seen a happier smile.

I remembered the potato pieces she picked out of the mud and gave her a piece of the sausage I'd bought, at a black market price. A piece, did I say? No. All of it. I gave her the whole damn sausage. Did I say Fritz *wasn't* stupid?

CHIMNEY SWEEP

Someone was calling me: "Andrej, Andrej, is it you? Wait, please wait!"

I turned around. A child with a bundle bouncing on

her back was running down the road. I thought: someone badly needs a chimney sweep. Trying to get me before I start on my rounds. When she caught up, she was out of breath but that didn't stop her babbling: "Oh, it is you, Andrej, I'm so glad it's you, where are they? Did you see them? Are they close by?"

"Calm down, little girl," I said. "Tell me where you live and I'll be there, first thing. I'll have a glassful at the tavern, only one, and then—"

"Oh, no," she said, "it's not about ⌐ chimney. I don't live around here. I am Katarína. Don't you remember?"

Yes . . . I've seen her somewhere. But I go through many villages, to many homes . . .

"You came to our house often," she said. "The gray one, with the red-tiled roof. I used to sit in the walnut tree and watch you work. Remember? You know my Aunt Lena. I am Katarína, her niece."

"Oh, yes," I said, "so you are. I didn't recognize you . . . eh . . . like that."

She wore city shoes but otherwise was dressed like a local peasant girl in a wide, gathered skirt, a sheepskin vest, a flowered kerchief tied over her red hair.

"Where did you get the peasant clothes?" I asked.

"The what? Oh, from Mariška. They belong to her sister, to Milka."

"Mariška, Milka . . . who are they?"

"Oh, Andrej, tell me about them first, I can't wait to hear!"

"Tell you what? About whom?"

"About Aunt Lena and Uncle Teo. Where are they?"

"Where are they? What makes you think I know?"

"You do, Andrej, you're just teasing me. Are they back at the house? Did they send for me?"

A strange child. I always thought so, seeing her in the nut tree, singing to herself for hours.

"Andrej . . ."

Her voice broke. She let her bundle slide to the ground.

"Why would I know where your aunt and uncle are?" I asked her.

She shrugged. "I . . . I don't know. You get around, talk to people, hear things. Hasn't someone mentioned them? Try to remember. *Please!*"

That's funny, I was thinking, because there was no need to beg me. Had I heard about them, I would have remembered. I am looking for those damn Jews myself. It's not only chimneys need cleaning up; my country does. The gall of this one, strutting about freely in broad daylight!

"It's you who need to remember," I said. "Your aunt and uncle must have told you something when they left. They didn't just walk off and leave you on the road, did they?"

They told her they were going on a trip, she said, for ten days, two weeks at the most, but six months had gone by and there'd been no word from them.

"And you've been on the road all this time? All through the winter?"

She shook her head.

"Where were you?"

"I stayed in a village," she whispered. "With a peasant family."

"A peasant family!" I spat. "Which peasant family? Where? What's their name?"

She kept quiet.

"Answer me!"

She was trembling, her mouth squeezed in a tight, stubborn line. I dug my fingers into her shoulders and shook her till she broke down and told the whole story.

It's the Plčko family she's stayed with, in Klietky. Twenty crowns a day paid for two weeks in advance, with a promissory note to double the amount for each additional day.

"Greedy Judas worshippers," I cursed. "They do anything for money!"

"Oh, no!" the girl sobbed. "Mariška didn't know Aunt Lena was my real aunt. She thought I was an adopted Christian orphan. She made me leave her house the minute she found out the truth about me."

" 'Made me leave'!" I mumbled, disgusted. A good Slovak would have turned the Jewess over to the Hlinka Guard, but no, Mariška let her go. Helped her escape. Gave her peasant clothes to wear.

"Who brought you to the Plčkos'?" I asked. "Who told you about them?"

Again, the tight, stubborn line. I didn't bother this time. Soon she'll be talking as much as they want her to!

"And where are you off to now?"

"I don't know," she whimpered. "I'll keep going, looking for them."

You're not going anywhere, I was thinking, your search is over.

But how do I get her to follow me to the village, I wondered. She won't want to, now that she's frightened of me, and I can't carry her, kicking and screaming, all the way to Headquarters.

"Do you have food?"

"Some," she answered. "A sausage."

"That won't do," I told her, wondering where she got it. "If you want to find your aunt and uncle, you have a long way to go. One gets hungry, walking. I know from experience. Come with me to the village, and I'll help you get some food."

She shook her head.

"Why?" I laughed. "You're afraid of me, because I shouted? Ha, pay no attention, I meant no harm. You know me!"

She kept her head down. All I saw was the flowered pattern of her kerchief.

"I used to come to your house, didn't I? Your Aunt Lena was never stingy with the slivovitz. 'Have another, Andrej,' she'd say. 'It's cold working on the rooftops.' A nice woman, your aunt. Yes. Don't worry, we'll find her."

She glanced up.

I smiled and held out my hand. "Come along."

Her hand was still shaking as it moved toward mine. I was about to clasp it, but she pulled it back.

Very well, I decided, I'll go by myself. It'll take me twenty minutes to get there, a few more to make my report. If she stays here, so much the better. If not, we'll overtake her on wheels.

"If you'd rather," I said, "wait for me here. Sit down on this rock, I won't be long. I'll bring you bread, apples, and cheese."

She shrugged.

"I'll bring sweets, too. Poppy-seed cake."

Her head popped up like a mushroom after rain. "Poppy-seed cake?"

"Yes, yes! Warm from the oven, with walnuts and raisins. Like Aunt Lena used to make."

She moved closer to the rock.

"Will you wait?"

She nodded.

I started walking toward the village.

WEDDING GUEST

We were riding to my nephew's wedding, my seven younger children, my married son, his wife, and their three, my wife, my nephew's godparents, the schoolmistress; it was so crowded our arms and legs were dangling over the cart, but no matter. The bottle was going around, we were in good spirits, cracking jokes, singing. My wife and daughters were sitting on their starched finery, in beaded headdresses, with colored ribbons woven into their hair. Even the mares had garlands around their necks and colored beads strung around their ears and streamers braided into their tails.

We were but a short ride out of our village when my youngest starts squealing, "Hey, hey, stop the horses! Look everybody, there, it's alive!" My married son, in the coachman's seat, thought something happened—he tugged on the reins so hard those of us in the rear rolled off the cart. No matter. The ground was no longer muddy and not yet dusty. I brushed off whatever clung to my pants. By the time I got on my feet and straightened the feather in my hat, the children were clustered at the edge of the road shouting for the rest of us to come.

There was a girl sitting on a rock playing with a monkey. I've never seen a monkey, except in pictures, but I know the Gypsies keep them. This was a very small one, wrapped in a shawl, like a baby. A cute little thing. Lively, all the while moving, scratching itself behind the ears, waving to us, playing with the fringes on the shawl, hiding, then peeking to see if we were still watching. The children jumped with joy, dared each other to touch it, but each time they were about to, even the bravest ran off screaming.

Everyone was having a good time except the schoolmistress. She kept staring at the monkey, at the red-haired girl, and suddenly she clapped her hands for quiet, like she does in the classroom. "That's not a live monkey," she announced, "it's a puppet. A glove with a monkey head. That's all it is!" "It's alive, alive!" the children shouted. I winked at the teacher. I only meant to stop her spoiling it for the children, but she got me wrong, turned red, and argued the louder.

The girl was looking at us, red-eyed, her face stained with tears. Probably got a hiding from her Gypsy father, I was thinking, and came here to have a cry. I reached for the pouch inside my vest and tossed her a coin. "Remove the shawl," commanded the schoolmistress. "I want to see the monkey. All of it!" The girl let the shawl slide down her arm and we saw: the monkey's body was a glove slipped over her hand. The teacher looked at us like she was the only smart one and walked back to the cart. The children didn't. They were still interested. Now they wanted to put that glove over their hands, try the tricks. Some did well, even very well, I'd say, but none made the monkey look alive like the Gypsy girl did.

"Hey"—I leaned over to my wife—"let's take her with us to the wedding. It'll make good entertainment." My wife thought I was crazy. No matter. She often does. "You want our kids to catch her lice," she asked, "her fleas?" "They're no different from their own," I said. "Where will you put her and her bundle?" she fussed. "We're falling off the cart as it is!" I winked. "We'll dump the schoolmarm and take the Gypsy instead." Some of the children must have overheard and told the others because now all of them were hollering so I had to cover my ears. I don't know which made them happier, taking the girl or dumping their teacher, but they certainly liked the idea. "How would you like to come with us, little Gypsy?" I asked. She smiled. "We're going to a wedding. They will like your monkey. You'll make a hatful in coins." No, she said, she couldn't. She was waiting for someone. She had to stay.

The children didn't give up. There'll be hot sausages on rolls to eat, they shouted, and went on about cakes filled with apples, nuts, raisins, cinnamon, apricot jam . . . they told her no one would care how much she ate, she could fill her belly and her pockets as well. I could tell her mouth was watering. "There'll be dancing," I said, "and music. The best fiddlers on this side of the Tatra Mountains."

"Dancing," she echoed. "Music?" Her red-rimmed eyes suddenly sparkled. She jumped off the rock, stuffed the monkey inside her vest, threw the bundle over her shoulder. The children raced her to the cart, cheering. A wisp of a girl she was, the Gypsy; it didn't feel any more crowded with her along. The little ones were all around her, on top of her, you couldn't see the tip of the child's nose, but she didn't seem to mind.

Well, I thought as we rode off, the someone she promised to wait for will not find her. No matter. It takes a fool to trust a Gypsy.

GOD'S PLAN

"Look." Anka is pointing to a building standing alone. "That must be the orphanage."

Saint Katarína, what do I do? I don't want to get there and I don't want to keep walking. Can you help?

The light May drizzle feels good on my face, but my shoes are soaked from stepping into a puddle. And I am tired. The walk from the train station has been long and boring. No mountains or streams, no villages. Nothing but gray plowed fields. Even the clothing peasants wear in this region is drab, with little embroidery or color. They waddle past us, loaded with bundles; dark, clumsy, like the crows pecking at seeds among the furrows.

"K-R-M-A-N-O-V D-O-M L-A-S-K-Y." Anka spells the letters mounted on the white, square building. "Yes, that's it."

Dom Lasky, the Home of Love, stands two stories high behind a spiked iron fence. Across the road, halfway up a hill, is a cemetery.

"It says here"—Anka is looking at a rusty sign on a

lamppost—" 'Protestant Orphanage and Old Age Home, founded by the Krmanov family in the year . . .' "

I squeeze Anka's hand. She squeezes mine. "You'll be all right, Katarinka. You'll make new friends, and the Sisters will be kind to you."

I am hoping they won't take me. I want to go back with Anka, to her village.

"What will you tell them?"

"The truth. They have to know that they're taking a risk. If anyone finds out they're keeping a Jewish child—"

"But I'm *not* Jewish, Anka, you know I'm not! I believe in everything you taught me!"

"You had better keep quiet about that or they'll throw you out!"

"Why?"

"I told you, it's a *Protestant* orphanage. This is a Protestant region."

"They won't let me pray to the Blessed Virgin?"

"No. And don't ask them to!"

"Then why did you bring me here?"

No answer.

"*Why?* And if they won't take me, what then?"

"I don't know. You can't come back home with me."

I remember the pale faces of Anka's parents when they looked up from their dinner plates and saw me standing in the doorway. No, I can't go back with Anka. But what will I do if they won't have me in the orphanage? Keep walking on this road by myself? Stay in the cemetery? At midnight, graves will open. Bony fingers will grab for me, souls will flicker in the darkness, ghosts loom above the tombstones . . .

"Anka, let's go in."

She looks me over, straightens my kerchief, then pinches my cheeks, hard. "That's to give you color," she explains. "You look pale, they might think you're sick."

The gate is locked. Anka crosses herself, mumbles a prayer, and rings the bell.

A tall woman in a long, dark blue dress appears in the courtyard. Her starched white bonnet hugs her head like a shell. She pulls a large key from her apron pocket and opens the gate.

"Good afternoon to you, Sister."

"Welcome. You're bringing us an orphan?"

She smiles at me. I look away. Soon the Sister will know the truth about me and then she won't smile. She'll turn pale like Anka's mother and say, "Why did you bring her here? She'll get us into trouble. Take her away!"

Anka fidgets with her shawl. "There's a problem, Sister. May I talk with you?"

We follow the Sister across the courtyard. At the entrance are two women dressed in black. One, standing, is shouting and shaking her fist at someone I can't see. The other, seated on a stool, is mumbling something I can't understand. Her head is on crooked and her hands tremble in her lap like frightened nestlings. I clutch Anka's hand as we pass between them. We climb a flight of stairs, then walk down a long, dark corridor. The Sister stops in front of a door and turns to me. She is young, with bright red cheeks and dark eyebrows that meet in the center.

"I am Sister Mara. What's your name?"

I stare at the stone floor.

"It's all right," Anka says, "you can talk."

I can, but what name am I to say? My real name or the name written in my false papers?

"Don't keep the Sister waiting."

"Katarína," I mumble. My given name has not been changed.

"And how old are you, Katarína?"

"In two weeks I'll be ten."

"Well then, Katarína, wait here on this bench while I and . . . er . . ."

"I am Anka. Anna Karolína Krupčiková."

". . . while I and Miss Krupčiková have our talk."

Anka hands me my bundle. "Don't talk to anyone," she warns me. "Don't make a sound."

"Anna Karolína Krupčiková." I mouth the words as I watch the door close behind them. I haven't heard Anka call herself by her full name since she first came to us. We were in the kitchen having supper, Uncle Teo, Aunt Lena, cousin Pavel, and I, when we heard a knock. In the doorway stood a peasant girl with brown eyes and golden hair. I saw the bundle at her feet and thought this must be the new maid we were waiting for all afternoon.

"I'm Anka," she said. "Anna Karolína Krupčiková."

Aunt Lena stood up. "Welcome, Anka. We thought you weren't coming."

"The mare took sick," Anka said. "I walked."

Walked all the way from Nárobky, her village! Aunt Lena looked happy. This Anka was someone to keep a promise, a maid she could trust. And young. Jews were not allowed to have maids younger than forty, but in our region they weren't strict about that law.

The door opens—Sister Mara is coming. She hurries past me. Her cheeks are white, she isn't smiling now. I see her go down the stairway. Anka must be alone in that room. I want to go to her, but just when I'm ready to, the sound of footsteps stops me. Sister Mara is back with another Sister and a man in a black vest. They walk into the room and shut the door.

I close my eyes and try to get back to Aunt Lena. I imagine her baking bread, think about the good smells in our kitchen. But what I breathe is the hospital odor of this long, dark corridor.

I don't want to stay in this place! Holy Mother, why did you let Anka bring me here, to a Protestant orphanage? Are you angry with me? Why?

Shuffling, whispers. Two girls are tiptoeing down the hall. I press against the wall and hold my breath.

"Hey, look. A new girl!"

They come closer and stare at me. I stare at my muddy shoes.

"Look, Vlasta, she's got red hair and freckles."

They don't rub buttons for good luck, as they do where I come from. They don't say, "Phew, phew, phew," as in the Plčkos' village. These girls just look at me, at each other, and giggle.

"You coming to stay?"

I keep my mouth shut.

"What's your name? I'm Betka. I have no mother or father. Do you?"

She's little, a first-grader, maybe, with pale blue eyes and straw-colored hair.

"Well—*do* you?"

Jesus, please, make them go away.

"Why won't she answer me, Vlasta?"

Vlasta has chestnut hair and looks twice Betka's age. She has a long thick braid, the kind I always wanted.

"Where you from?"

Patron Saint, help!

"How old are you?"

I'll make a sign—show ten fingers. That won't make a sound. But is that the age written in the false papers? I don't remember. My fingers stay out of sight, scraping the underside of the bench.

"Tell us your name," Vlasta commands. "Or don't you know it?"

My face is burning.

"You don't?" Vlasta tosses her braid over her other shoulder. "Hey, Betka, have you heard such a thing? The new girl doesn't know her name."

"There's one like that where I come from. A dummy."

"Maybe she's one, too. Can you hear?" Vlasta asks me. I nod.

Her eyes narrow. "Then why don't you answer. You're too good for us?"

I shake my head.

"Stuck-up scarecrow!"

"Stuck-up." Betka sticks out her tongue at me.

"Too stupid to talk. She grew up in a pigpen, with pigs."

"With pigs," Betka echoes. "Oink, oink."

"She's got shit spots on her face to show for it. See?"

"Yeah, shit spots—"

The door swings open. "Vlasta! Betka! Get back to the study at once."

Sister Mara claps her hands as if shooing a pair of geese. The girls scuttle down the hall.

"Did you tell them anything?"

I shake my head.

"Good. Don't talk. Not a word to anyone."

She goes back to the room. I clench my fist, pound the bench. A dummy, they call me. Stuck-up. It's she that's stuck-up, Vlasta, tossing her fat braid this way, that way, showing off. Raised in a pigpen? I wish she'd come back, I'd tell her where I was raised. I'm sick of keeping my mouth shut. Sick of it. If I keep it shut any longer, my lips will grow together. For three days I had to grunt, whimper, talk with my hands. Anka's stupid idea. "The child is a deaf-mute," she told them on the train. "I'm taking her to an institution." The next thing, a stork flies out of a swamp. "Look, Anka," I shouted, "look at the stork." Anka's eyes bulged. Everyone else's dropped. They stared at their shoes, fumbled with their bundles. Anka pulled me down the corridor to another compartment, but still she worried that someone would report us. Her hands shook each time she handed my papers over for inspection.

You'd have been scared silly, Vlasta. Peed in your pants. A few hours by train, Anka said. It took us three days to get here. That's because lots of bridges and tunnels are blown up. Partisans are doing that, they're trying to save our country. Don't believe what people are saying—they don't have horns and long, black tails. My cousin, Pavel, is as handsome as a prince from a fairy tale and he is a partisan. It's a secret Anka told me today, when we got off the train.

We had to wait for ferries, walk over mountains. Every time we neared a bridge that wasn't blown up yet, all talk stopped. The train would creep like a snail and everyone would sit as if they had turned to stone, only their lips moving. Mumbling prayers to Saint Ján of Nepomuk. But once on the other side, jabber jabber. All tongues would let loose. All but mine.

Ask anything you want, Betka, I'm talking. You have no mother or father. I don't either. My parents died in an avalanche, in the Tatra Mountains. But that's not why I'm here. I have Aunt Lena, who's like a mother to me. Anka brought me because—uh—she's in that room, telling the Sisters and the man in the black vest why she did. She's asking them to keep me here, but they might not want to—they'd be taking a risk.

Anka is Catholic. I am, too. I believe everything she taught me. We went to Mass together every Sunday.

Aunt Lena knew. She didn't know I stopped in church every day on my way from school, that I spent my allowance on candles, that I picked flowers from our garden—ones I wasn't supposed to—to take to shrines along the road.

I don't know where Aunt Lena is. She and Uncle Teo went on a trip and I was to wait for them at the Plčkos'. Aunt Lena told them I was a Catholic orphan, but someone found out the truth and told Mariška, the oldest daughter. I had to leave. At dawn, Mariška walked me on the footpath behind the barns to the outskirts of the village. We both cried. "God be with you, Katarína," she said. "I'll be praying for you."

I started walking to the next village. Then the next, and the next. I did house chores for a meal, and sometimes they'd let me spend the night by the kitchen stove. Or I'd sneak into a barn. I don't know how many days went by.

One morning I met Andrej, the chimney sweep from my village. He was covered with soot from head to toe, but I was so glad to see him I flung my arms around him. Andrej knew my aunt and uncle—I thought he'd have news of them. When I asked, his face turned ugly. He spat. Even his spittle was black. "You tell *me* where they are," he shouted. "I bet you know!" He dug his fingers into my shoulders, wouldn't stop shaking me. "You'll talk, little one. You will."

Then suddenly, his mood changed. He said he'd help me find Aunt Lena. He told me to wait, he'd bring me bread, apples, poppy-seed cake. I nodded but didn't promise.

After he left, I sat on a rock, pulled my monkey puppet out of my bundle, slipped her over my hand. "Don't be frightened, Stefie," I told her. "Andrej won't harm us, he is bringing us sweets, all the things you like . . ." Some villagers riding by in a cart thought I was a Gypsy girl talking to a real monkey. They were going to a wedding and took us along.

The wedding was fun. People kept telling me, "Eat, little Gypsy, there's plenty, no need to steal, take all you want." I didn't mind being taken for a Gypsy girl, they're pretty. And I did eat my bellyful. Filled my pockets with cookies and nuts, stuffed two raisin loaves into my bundle. But when the last cart left at dawn, there I was, on my own again. "Blessed Mother," I prayed, "what do I do? Where do I go?" I set out to look for a place where the Virgin might appear. There, I thought, if I prayed long enough, hard enough, she would talk to me or give me a sign.

I knew the right place the minute I saw it—it was like the ones on the holy picture cards Anka gave me: a clearing half-hidden by pines, with a spring trickling over rocks. I knelt with my rosary and started on the Hail Marys.

The first time through, nothing happened. Then, on the last bead the second time around, I felt it—a chill in my head, goose bumps creeping up my arms, a hum in my ears, all the feelings I get when she is close. At the same time a little yellow bird started chirping. I listened. Was it telling me something? "Help me find my nest, I lost my way, I lost it . . ." The words kept turning over in my head. Where did they come from, a song? No, a poem. A poem Anka taught me, about a nightingale. "I sing by night, I weep by day, oh, help me find my way . . ." I imagined Anka reciting it, heard her voice, she was there with me, so real I could feel her breath, smell the chamomile buds she uses to rinse her hair. That was it: the bird was my sign from the Virgin, it was telling me what to do. I was to go to Anka. She was back in Nárobky with her family.

I started walking. No, running, and I hardly stopped to rest. Anka used to take me to Nárobky in the summer, on her days off. Father Krupčik, in his Sunday suit, would be looking out for us on the road. Mother Krupčiková would be in the kitchen, piling plates of cakes on the table. Anka's brothers and sisters—Leo, Petík, Batko, Cilka, Lydia—Krupčiks of all sizes, they'd be as excited as I was. We'd swing on ropes in the barn, jump off the ladder into a pile of hay, ride their mare bareback, chase one another, wrestle. There'd be a calf to pet and kittens to play with and little yellow chicks to cradle in my hands. Tonight, I thought, I'd make them laugh—put on a show with Stefie.

It was dark by the time I got to Anka's house. I crouched under the window and peered inside. The family sat around the table, eating supper. An oil lamp flickered, throwing shadows on the wall, lighting up one face, then another. There was Anka, her golden hair falling over her shoulders. Leo and Petík were heaping steaming potatoes on their plates—my stomach rumbled at the sight. Lydia, with a buttermilk mustache, was feeding little Batko. Father Krupčik's head was bowed, I saw his face from the side only. Mother Krupčiková's back was to the window.

What a surprise when they'll see me! In my mind I was already hugging them, squeezing myself on a seat between Anka and Lydia, stuffing my mouth with potatoes and bacon chips. I turned the corner, ducked under the side window, tiptoed up the steps, and slowly, softly opened the door.

"Katarína!" Lydia jumped to her feet. Her father looked up, hushed her. Why was he staring at me like that, didn't he recognize me? Mother Krupčiková turned around. "Ježiš Mária," she whispered, crossing herself. "How the child looks! What are you doing here? What do you want?"

My knees wobbled. I couldn't hold back the tears. Anka rushed over, hugged me, kept saying how happy she was to see me. I asked about Aunt Lena and Uncle Teo and she said, no, she hadn't heard from them, the last time she did was before Christmas. "And Pavel?" I asked. Did she know where he was? Yes, Anka whispered in my ear, she'd tell me, but not now. Over her words I could hear her parents saying, "She can't stay here, she'll get us in trouble, someone might see, hear, report . . ."

Anka pleaded. Would they turn out a hungry child?

Would they let her roam the village streets, at night, by herself? And this wasn't just any child, it was Katarína, a friend, often a welcome guest in their home. She was in danger, in need of help. Would they shut their door? Let them look into their Christian souls, their loving hearts. Would they?

Her father gave in. "All right, for two days. In the hayloft."

Two days stretched into two weeks while Anka tried to get me false papers.

"Learn your new name, Katarínka. Your birth certificate says you are Katarína Zemanová. A good Slovak name. And your religion is Protestant."

"What's that?" I didn't want to be Protestant, not even on false papers. "Take it back, Anka. I'm Catholic."

"We're lucky to have it," she said. "It's hard to get and not cheap. The price of three fat geese."

"Anka, for an extra chicken, would they change the religion to—"

"No, they wouldn't. Listen, Katarínka. I'm taking you to an orphanage."

"An orphanage! Where?"

"It's a few hours from here—"

"That's too far. How will Aunt Lena find me?"

"I'll tell her where you are."

"And will you visit often, Anka? Promise?"

"I can't promise that, Katarínka, but you'll be back soon. The minute the war is over."

"When will you tell me where Pavel is? You said you would."

"I will after we leave here."

"When is that?"

"Tomorrow."

"Are we walking?"

"No, we're going by train."

"Oh, good. I love to ride on trains."

Anka's parents begged her not to go. They talked about partisans blowing up tunnels and bridges, trains plunging into ravines, people buried alive under mountains. "They catch you with those false papers and you're done for. Charged with treason for helping the enemy."

Anka was deaf to their warnings. In the morning she had Petik harness the mare to take us to the train station in the nearest town. While we rode through her village, I was wrapped in a blanket, like a mummy, and laid flat in the cart, under straw.

We stayed at the far end of the platform, away from the others. I held Anka's hand, my eyes looking for white puffs of smoke, for a dark little dot to appear far down the tracks. I loved to watch that dot grow into a huge, hissing monster. It gave me gooseflesh each time.

Anka squeezed my hand. "Remember, you're a deaf-mute," she whispered. "I don't want you talking to people or having them ask you questions. You don't hear, you don't talk."

I nodded. I didn't know how hard that would be. Sometimes I needed to talk so badly I'd tug Anka by the sleeve and we'd wobble down the corridor, to the toilet. Inside, with the wheels clattering, she'd let me talk. Lots of times I'd cry instead. Anka would tell me not to, to think about the saints, their courage and faith. "Trust in God, Katarínka. If he is making you suffer, it's for a reason. God has a plan . . ."

"Whose are you?"

A woman with a mop and pail is standing in front of me, looking me over.

"Where you from?"

I feel my mouth twitching.

"Don't cry, little one, the Sisters are good. They'll take care of you till the day you marry."

She shuffles down the hall. "The poor thing," I hear her mumble. "Red hair and freckles. The Lord knows who'll have her . . ."

Who'll have me? Pavel will, you silly. And I won't be staying here long—I'll be going home the minute the war is over.

Little Betka, will she stay here until she marries? Grow up in this dark, stinky place? Does she know what it's like to live in a house, with a room of her own, with her own Aunt Lena?

It must be terrible to be an orphan—*and* Protestant. If she were Catholic, at least she'd have a mother in heaven. She does anyway, but doesn't know it. Someone needs to tell her, tell her about the Holy Mother, the saints . . . then she wouldn't look so sad and pale . . . she'd feel as if she had a big family with lots of aunts and uncles watching over her—and a patron saint to herself, one she didn't have to share.

Jesus, you sent Anka to save me—send someone to
save Betka. Vlasta, too. All the children in this orphanage.
Remember what you said about a good shepherd and
stray sheep? These children are like lost lambs. Like the
lost lamb I was, in Anka's dream. Someone needs to tell
them about the holy family, the saints, the fifteen mysteries, the Holy Sacraments, someone . . . someone . . .
Jesus! Is that why I am here? You want me to do it? Me,
by myself? Holy saints! Is that why you had Anka bring
me here? Why Aunt Lena didn't come back yet and
Mariška made me leave? Is that why everything turned
out the way it did?

Saint Katarína, did you know about this? Will you help
me? You must. It's lucky I brought the holy picture
cards—Anka told me not to, but I did—they're in my
bundle inside a sock. I know the stories about saints and
miracles, know Catholic songs and prayers, I have the
questions and answers from the catechism memorized.
Dear Patron Saint, stay with me, don't leave me for a
minute. We'll do our work in secret, when the Sisters
are asleep. I wish we could keep it secret from the
Blessed Mother, too, surprise her on Assumption Day.
Wouldn't that make a wonderful gift? She'll be sitting on
her throne, all dressed up for the holiday, and she'll hear
children's voices singing "Ave Maria." She'll look down,
and what a surprise—those voices will be coming from
a Protestant orphanage . . .

"No, Sister. Krmanov's Home of Love cannot shut its
door to a child—"

"What about the other children in our trust? Our duty is to them."

"Our duty is to *all* children, and let's not forget charity, compassion, love . . ."

They're shouting in that room, trying to make up their minds. They don't know it's not up to them. Jesus wants me here. It is God's plan.

I am scared, but happy, too. The Holy Mother isn't angry with me; she wants me to pray to her. Here is the rosary, in my pocket. How lucky this skirt has a deep pocket, that way I can feel the little beads whenever I want to—even during the Protestant prayers the Sisters will make me say. It won't matter. In my heart I'll be saying my own, and soon I won't be the only one. There'll be Vlasta, Betka, all the girls in the orphanage praying with me, "Hail Mary, full of grace, the Lord is with thee . . ."

KRMANOV'S HOME OF LOVE

How can I save the orphans, Jesus, if they won't talk to me?

Sister Mara says I shouldn't mind, it takes a few days before the children talk to a new orphan. But it doesn't stop at that. At mealtimes no one wants to sit next to me—those closest pinch their noses shut and turn away.

It's the turpentine. The day I came, Sister Mara tried to run a fine comb through my hair. I screamed. So did she: "Katarína, you're swarming with lice!" She had me sit on a stool while she rubbed my scalp with cotton dunked in turpentine. I, too, pinched my nose shut. The turpentine stinks and makes my eyes burn.

When she was done, the Sister wound a towel around my head. "Now I'll take you to the study," she said, "to meet the children."

I stood up. In the bathroom mirror I saw a Turk in a yellow turban with very red eyes and a red, shiny nose. "Oh, no!" I cried. "I don't want anyone to see me like this.

Please, Sister, let me hide somewhere!" She laughed. She said that all the orphans have lice when they come to Krmanov's Home of Love. I gripped the faucet, but she pried my fingers loose and dragged me, shrieking, into the study.

"This is Katarína Zemanová." I heard myself introduced by my new, made-up name. "She is an orphan from Uhovce."

In the dim light I could see the children sitting at a table that ran the length of the room. No one moved or made a sound.

"Put your notebooks away and set the table for supper. Be nice to Katarína, let her help you."

Sister Mara left. I felt eyes fasten on me, like pins. I stood with my back against the door. A butterfly pinned to a board.

"Turpentine!" someone shouted. "The new girl has lice."

"Get her out of here, she stinks!"

"Uhovce! Did you hear? She grew up with pigs."

"Those are shit spots all over her face."

"Who'll sit next to her at supper?"

"Not me!"

"Not me!"

"Not me!"

Everyone was shouting. They reached for tin bowls on a shelf and started banging on them with spoons. I ducked and covered my ears, but the noise grew louder. They were closing in on me. "Saint Katarína," I whispered, pressing against the door, "save me!"

The door gave way. I felt myself sinking into folds of blue.

"Are you awake?"

I am lying on a narrow bed in a small, tidy room. Sister Mara is shaking a thermometer.

"You fainted, Katarína. I brought you to my room."

I remembered the study. Children banging on tin bowls. My prayer to Saint Katarína. Once again she saved me.

"Did you dream about your aunt? You were calling her."

"Yes, Sister." In my dream I saw a village. Below was the red-tiled roof of our house. Our garden. But everything in it looked enormous —tulips tall as trees, daisies and daffodils broad enough to sit on. In the kitchen, Aunt Lena and Anka were setting the table. "Aunt Lena," I cried, "I am back, let me in!" She didn't hear me. "Aunt Lena," I shouted, beating against the windowpane, "it's me, Katinka."

She looked up and smiled. "Look, Anka," she said, pointing at me. "What a pretty butterfly."

I want to write a secret diary, but the only place I can be alone is in the old, half-collapsed shed. And not for long, or I am missed.

My bed is by the window. When the moon gets fuller, I'll be able to write in bed after lights out and look at my pictures of saints. No one will see. The mattress is like a hammock: it sags in the center where the straw's been worn to a fine dust. My back is sore from rubbing against the bedsprings.

The girls are still not talking to me. Jesus, remember the surprise I thought of for your Mother? Protestant orphan girls singing "Ave Maria" on Assumption Day? Get the girls to talk to me, please, or we'll never be ready!

I hate this place. It smells like a hospital. Looks like one, too. The girls' dormitory could be a ward with its ten beds on one side, eight on the other, and everything white. No embroideries hanging on the white walls, no pictures. Oh, yes—*one*! I try not to look at it, but it looks at me, in every room. An angry man with crazy eyes. "Who is that?" I asked Sister Mara the day I came. "Is it Mr. Krmanov?" She dropped the fine comb she was trying to run through my hair and wrung her hands. "Good Lord, it's lucky no one heard you. Who'd believe you're Protestant if you don't recognize Martin Luther?"

Martin Luther. That's who these poor orphans get to look at. But not for much longer. Mad Martin will come off the walls and instead there'll be the beautiful, gentle faces of saints. In our dorm, Saint Agneša, patron of young girls. In the study, Saint Beňadik, patron of school-children. Saint Marta in the kitchen. Saint Hieronym, patron of orphans, in the hall.

Whenever I can, I sneak out to the shed to kneel at my imaginary shrine of the Blessed Virgin. After a while the musty smell inside doesn't bother me. I say my prayers and breathe the scents of candles, incense, and roses.

. . .

The bell wakes us mornings at six. By seven we are combed and dressed and have our beds made. The bathroom has a trough with six faucets. The oldest girls, twelve to fourteen years of age, get ready first, then help the little ones. We hurry to get to the study before the boys do. I don't know why.

For breakfast we have porridge and malt coffee, with dry bread. From eight to ten we do cleaning chores.

Our lessons start at ten-fifteen. Brother Martin sits at the head of the long table and dictates from the only textbook we have in each subject. We learn Slovak history, grammar, arithmetic, and religion. Afternoons we memorize from our copybooks what Brother Martin dictated in the morning.

At noon the two Sisters bring a large pot of food into the study. We line up with our tin bowls for one ladleful each. At four o'clock we line up again with tin cups, for more of the breakfast drink and a slice of bread with a tiny bit of lekvar, the prune jam that Božena used to slather on her bread two centimeters thick. Then, until it gets too dark to see, the girls sit around a large basket of clothes and pick things to patch, darn, or mend. The electric light is not turned on in the study till after supper.

Whenever she can, Sister Mara calls me into her room to teach me Protestant prayers and hymns I'm supposed to know. I don't like learning them, but it's nice to be with Sister Mara in her neat little room.

I asked her to keep Stefie for me. I have no place to hide her in the dorm, and can't talk to her nights, anyway, with all the girls around. I never go to the room of the other Sister, Sister Johanna. She doesn't like me. I don't like her, either.

After supper there is a short service. The last bell, for lights-out, rings at eight-thirty.

Under the covers I feel the beads of my rosary and pray to the Holy Virgin. Then, until I fall asleep, I imagine I am home waiting for Aunt Lena to come kiss me good night.

It's Saturday. Bath time. The girls are lined up in threes. The next three waiting to get into the tub have to take their clothes off. I look away.

I think of Saturday baths at home: the fire crackling in the stove, the large bathroom steamy hot . . . me soaking in the scented suds, singing, not wanting to get out, ever . . .

Three girls get out of the tub. The next three get in. Sister Johanna, the cook, and another helper wash one girl each. Their faces are red from racing each other. Ready, set, go: Hand. Foot. Underarms. Behind the ears. Bottoms of feet. Belly buttons, knees. Rags rubbed with hard brown soap scrub over buttocks, over faces. The girls cry out, squeeze their eyes shut against the burning soap, turn their heads away, but nothing slows down the washers.

Aunt Lena would let me wash myself. She'd come in

only to add hot water, scrub my back, and in the end, to wash my hair. The last rinse, chamomile buds soaked in rainwater . . .

"Hurry up, Katarina, get undressed. Marta, Betka, and you are next."

I don't move. I will not stand here naked in front of all the girls.

The large, terrycloth robe . . . Aunt Lena would wrap me in it, rub me dry . . . face, neck, ears, gently . . . then all over roughly enough to leave my body pink and tingling. The scent of chamomile would—

"Hey, what's wrong with you?" Sister Johanna, hands on hips, is glaring at me. "Don't you like to bathe?"

The water is black. It must be cold by now because the girls who got out are shivering and their lips are blue.

"Answer me, girl."

"Yes," I mumble. "In clean water. By myself."

She squints. Her mouth turns crooked. "Excuse me, Your Highness. I forget how special you are."

She grabs me by the wrist, marches me down the hall, and pushes me into the dorm. "Here. By yourself. And no supper."

I hear the key turn in the lock. I am crying, but after a while it feels good to be alone. I'm never alone except for the few minutes I manage to sneak away to the shed. Now I can take the holy picture cards out of the mattress where I hide them and spread them over the bed.

For the first time since I came to the orphanage I am looking in daylight at all those faces I love. I wish the orphans could be here looking at them with me and loving them, too.

Jesus, why aren't you helping me?
.

A girl talked to me today. Her name is Olga. Olga says the other girls hate her because she stutters. She is one of the older ones—about to turn thirteen—and she wants to be my friend.

I am so happy!

Tomorrow I'll be ten years old. I dreamed I was back home, celebrating.

On my last birthday, Aunt Lena filled the house with lilacs. They grew along the fence and were in full bloom this time of year; I'd feel the moist clusters brush against my cheek each time I walked through the squeaky garden gate.

On May 16 Aunt Lena would always let me sleep late, even on a school day. She'd bring me my favorite breakfast in bed—a cup of cocoa with whipped cream and poppy-seed cake.

In the afternoon she'd let me invite friends, and we'd have chocolate cake she baked, ice cream, and soda water with raspberry syrup. Aunt Lena wouldn't allow the children to bring presents or have me show them ones I got from her. "Remember, Katinka," she'd say, "most of the children are poor. Their parents can't get them gifts such as you get."

I'd get my gifts the night before, after dinner. There'd be books, games, puzzles, notebooks to color, sometimes

a new dress, and last year, the very best present ever—
Stefie. This morning I woke up to the scent of lilacs. I
don't want to let it go . . .

Yesterday I was hurting all day. I missed Aunt Lena and
home more than ever.

I told Olga it was my birthday. She shrugged, said, "So
what?" I guess no one ever made a fuss over hers.

After supper, Sister Mara sent for me. She said,
"Katarina, you're ten years old. Congratulations. I'm
sure you're used to getting presents—our children get
gifts only for Christmas." She pulled out of her apron
pocket something wrapped in a napkin. "I saved you a
piece of cake," she told me. "Eat it here, in my room,
and don't talk about it." I burst out crying because—
yes—I was homesick, but also because I love Sister Mara
so much.

Sister Johanna sent for me. Did that strange man I saw
talking to her bring a message from Aunt Lena? I break
into a run.

But when I get to the office the man isn't there. Sister
Johanna is shouting at Sister Mara, "I told you it wouldn't
work, truth won't hide behind a false name. It shows
in everything—her speech, manners, expressions—and
you"—she turns to me—"what do you think you're
doing? You want to get us into trouble?"

I look at Sister Mara for help, but she says nothing.

"You are supposed to be an orphan from Uhovce.
Don't you understand?"

"She doesn't," Sister Mara answers for me. "She's never been there."

Sister Johanna glares at her. "It was a silly choice. Did you think a girl with her background could pass for some primitive—"

"Yes, it was a mistake, Sister, I am sorry. The day she came to us Katarína pointed to a picture of Martin Luther and asked if he was Mr. Krmanov. Her ignorance of Protestantism worried me. I thought I'd have her come from the hinterlands. A place like Uhovce."

"There is a lesson for you, Katarína. One lie leads to another until you trip, and then God help you! In Uhovce people slurp their soup and they haven't heard of the alphabet."

I shrug. That's not my fault. Why is Sister Johanna scolding *me*?

"I felt as if *liar* were written in capitals across my forehead," she tells Sister Mara. "He sees her coming out of the shed—what were you doing there, Katarína?—and asks who she is. 'An orphan from Uhovce, Inspector,' I tell him. 'Primitive, you know.' I thought that, seeing me with a stranger, the girl would have sense enough to disappear, but no. She saunters over to introduce herself. 'I am Katarína,' she says, and curtsies, like a duchess. Then runs ahead to hold the door open for us. I felt my cheeks turning red but had to think quickly of another lie to cover up the first, may the Lord forgive me. 'We're teaching the girls manners, Inspector,' I told him. 'Katarína is practicing her lesson.' "

Sister Mara laughs. "A fine idea, Sister. They should be learning manners."

"A fine idea, yes. We'll teach our girls to curtsy while the front is closing in."

I can't wait to tell Aunt Lena that *good* manners got me into trouble. And I must remember to slurp my soup.

Today Betka talked to me. She says the others are ready to as well, but not while I am still friends with Olga.

What do I do, Jesus? I know you want to help, but do I have to turn my back on Olga? You didn't like it when Saint Peter turned his back on you. Think of some other way, please.

"Olga, stop pushing!"

"W-we were here f-first."

"So what? You never have any visitors. You and your friend with the shit spots. The pigs from Uhovce coming to see her?"

Olga and I are jostling for space along the fence. Vlasta's elbow is digging into my ribs, but I won't let go of the iron bars. I squeeze my face between the railings and watch the road.

Sundays the dorms stay unlocked. We are allowed to take visitors upstairs to sit on our beds. Ones like Olga and me who never have visitors stand around and ogle the gifts coming out of baskets and bundles: cinnamon buns, candy, nuts, apples, colored ribbons, pencils. Later, some of the gifts are traded. Jožko, the half-Gypsy, will carve a flute for a sausage. Olga copies two pages of homework for a licorice stick. If Vlasta would talk to me, I'd do any of her morning chores for a piece of that poppy-seed cake her aunt brings. I'd give Šebesta, the bed-wetter, my share of Sunday's butter for one dried apricot.

Olga stays downstairs, waiting. She doesn't have relatives but thinks her guardian might come. Or someone from her village might remember her.

I love Sister Mara. To be near her, I volunteer for extra chores. I am happiest working in the kitchen, where I can smell and taste the good food. *Their* food.

Six days a week there are two large pots on the stove, one for the orphanage, the other for the old-age home: Mondays it's beans; Tuesdays, squash. Wednesdays, turnips. Thursdays, peas. Fridays, lentils. Saturdays, noodles with cabbage. Sundays we eat cold food—tea and bread with butter.

The food I like to taste and smell isn't in the large pots—it's simmering in little ones: creamed vegetables, sauces, gravies, stewed fruit. And sometimes, roasting in the oven, is a chicken, duck, ham, rabbit, or venison, offerings people bring from their farms or from a hunt. *Their* food is what the cook makes for herself and the staff.

Smelling the good food makes me do crazy things—I burn my fingers dipping them into boiling gravies, scorch my throat and tongue on cookies snatched off a baking pan. Sister Mara makes believe she doesn't see, but I know that she does. When the cook isn't around, she lets me "clean out" those little pots and bowls before dipping them into soapy water in the sink.

Sister Mara loves me. On Fridays, when I clean her room, I often find a surprise she left for me—an apple or a sweet. And for doing two hours of extra chores on Saturdays, she lets me take a bath in clean water, by myself.

Two weeks after Olga and I became friends, she is gone. Her guardian sent for her. He thinks that, having turned thirteen, she is old enough to go into domestic service. I miss her. Once again I have no one to talk to. But Olga said she'd visit me Sundays if she didn't have to work. Now I, too, have someone to wait for.

Poor Olga, she wouldn't look when I tried to show her my saints. She was afraid the Sisters would find out. I told her she needn't worry, it is God's plan. But she shook her head all the same.

Sister Johanna ordered us girls to the barn to fill our mattresses with fresh straw. The mattresses are burlap bags closed on both ends, with a slit in the center for stuffing in the straw. Before we left she said, "Remember, first turn those bags inside out and shake out the old straw."

I am shaking mine when a flock of colored birds soars above my head. I freeze. Fluttering in the air are the holy picture cards I've kept hidden inside my mattress. Seconds later, the haloed heads lie scattered all over the barn. Saint Uršula, Saint Veronika, and Saint Sebastian lie at my feet, Saint Terézia at Betka's. Saint Katarína is sliding down Marta's nose, Saint Peter rests on Vlasta's shoulder. Wherever I look, saints' eyes are gazing at me from emptied burlap bags and heaps of straw.

I am too stunned to move. So are the girls, but not for long. The next thing they're elbowing each other to get at the cards, pouncing on them. "Bring all of those silly pictures here, to me," Vlasta commands. "I'm taking them to the office to show Brother Martin and the Sisters."

But she doesn't leave with my secret treasures right then. I guess she wants to look at all of them first.

I am pretending to study, but I can't think of anything except of what happened this morning in the barn. At any minute the door will open. I'll be called to the office and told to get out of Krmanov's Home of Love.

Jesus, please give me another chance.

He did.

I had stuffed too much straw into my mattress, and that made it slope from the center slit down. No sooner did I close my eyes at night than I rolled off the bed.

The girls made fun of me, but not for long. They, too, started falling off their sloping mattresses. Every few minutes we heard a thud as one of us landed on the floor. Betka kept score. I led by a wide margin. The straw filling was meant to protect my back from the bedsprings. Instead, it was throwing me out of my bed.

We laughed so hard that two girls peed in their beds. Vlasta forgot she wasn't talking to me and came over to help me flatten my mattress. We pushed the straw toward the four corners and beat the center part until it was level. "Here," she said, handing back my holy picture cards. "I won't tell on you if you'll tell us about the saints."

The other girls followed Vlasta to my bed. I started by telling them the story of Saint Katarína, my patron saint.

THE WAR

Today we taped blackout paper over all the windowpanes so the airplanes won't see light when they come to bomb. Brother Martin said those were just regulations, no one would want to bomb an orphanage, but I worry. How could a pilot, so high up, read the sign on our building that says KRMANOV'S HOME OF LOVE?

Now that the children are talking to me, they ask questions I don't know how to answer. No one believes I come from Uhovce.

One of the boys, Šebesta, the bed-wetter, asked if I was Jewish. His uncle is a government official. On the Sundays he visits, the uncle always wears the Hlinka Guard uniform.

The girls like the idea of surprising the Blessed Mother on Assumption Day, August 15. We have lots of time to get ready—Vlasta counted ten weeks. Evenings we're saying the Hail Marys together, but there is only one rosary, mine, to go around. Marta, the lame orphan, had a good idea. We are going to sneak some kernels of corn and dried beans out of storage and string them. Maybe we'll soak them first—to make them soft. Each set of ten kernels will be separated by a bean. There'll be enough rosaries for each girl to have one of her own.

Once a week, on Sundays for supper, there is butter on the table. It's brought up the back stairway so that the old people won't see it. Sister Mara said they haven't tasted or seen butter since the war started.

Some of the people in the old-age home aren't old. They are there because they're crazy and have no place else to go. Like Samuel. All day he sits quietly by the door, but I can tell there is something wild inside him. Vlasta said that when Samuel starts howling and thrashing, it takes five men to hold him down. His eyes are bright green, like a cat's. Each time I pass Samuel's chair, I expect him to leap at me.

Kača is crazy, too, but I am not afraid of her. Her shouting is less frightening than Ratenica's laughter. Then there are some who are too weak, or sick, to get out of bed. Cross-eyed Cupek cries all day like a baby. Old Hrnec keeps tapping rhythms on the two teeth he has left. Helen's head is on crooked and never stops shaking.

Sundays after supper we go downstairs to the old-age home for the evening service. Brother Martin leads the prayers. I mouth them, but in my heart I am saying Catholic prayers, my rosary dangling under the table.

When hymn-singing starts, Vlasta and I can barely keep straight faces—Kača shrieks, Ratenica laughs, Cupek snivels, old Mr. What's-his-name croaks like a frog, Mad Magdaléna sings tunes of her own!

After the service it's bedtime. We wait for lights-out, and then, in as loud a whisper as I dare, I tell the girls about the Holy Mother and the saints. They love the cards and the stories, and I think they like sharing a secret to keep from the Sisters.

I am in Brother Martin's office. His eyes sparkle. His face is red.

"Katarína, sit down. I have news you'll be very happy to hear." I jump to my feet. From whom, what, when, I want to know. A message, a note?

He looks at me, surprised, then sighs. "The news is not from your family, child, it's about the war." He leans close and whispers, "Allied forces have landed in Normandy."

I swallow hard. This is not the news I'd hoped to hear. What are Allied forces? Where is Normandy? Instead of asking, I smile. But Brother Martin reads my mind.

"Allied forces are fighting Germany, same as the Russians." His voice is barely above a whisper. "They are British, American, Canadian—from countries far away, but they've come to Normandy. They're in France, Katarína, no longer far from us. These armies are on our side, they . . ."

Our side. That's what is so confusing. Slovakia sides

with Germany. If the Germans lose the war, so does Slovakia. Would Brother Martin want his own country to lose?

"This is very good news, Katarína. The war can't last much longer. You won't have to hide anymore."

News that needs to be whispered comes from the forbidden radio station. Brother Martin could go to prison for listening to it. How very much he trusts me. How sure he is that he can. What if he knew that I had wanted to go to Hitler's birthday party? That I had cheered along with my classmates each time our principal, Rospačil, announced that "yet another country has fallen before the German might"?

"I'll ask the Sisters to assign you office work once a week. That way I can keep you informed. If anything very special happens, I'll send for you. Now go back to the study and don't let the good news show on your face."

I don't go to the study. I need to be by myself, to think. I go to the shed.

Jews are enemies of the Slovak state. Everyone knows that. We're taught it in school, we hear it on the radio, at rallies, in the streets, it's printed in newspapers, scribbled on walls, painted on billboards and placards. I used to resent my aunt and uncle for wanting the Russians to win the war. It made them the enemies of my country the Jews were said to be.

Brother Martin is Christian. He loves Slovakia. Yet he,

too, wants the Russians to win. Could someone want that and still be a good Slovak?

I told Brother Martin that I cried for days when the Hlinka Youth would not have me as a member.

"Katarína, I can't believe my ears," he said.

"I thought that—um—I wanted to be a good Slovak."

He shook his head. "Poor child, you were well taught what to think. I assumed that your aunt and uncle explained things to you, but they were right not to. It would have been dangerous for them and you."

I asked him how he could love his country and at the same time want it to lose the war.

"Country isn't the same as politics, Katarína. Many Slovaks don't agree with our government for siding with Germany. Some have joined the Russian partisans in the mountains and are fighting for a—"

"My cousin, Pavel, is a partisan," I blurted out; I felt it was all right for Brother Martin to know.

"God bless him. Let's pray for your cousin, Katarína. Pray for all the brave men and women fighting for a free Czechoslovakia. May God protect them."

The day Brother Martin whispered about Allied forces in Europe he warned me, "Don't let the good news show on your face." One look at his, and I can tell which way the war is going. On Good News Days (GND) his face glows, he jokes with us, bounds up the stairs two at a time. On Bad News Days (BND) he frowns, grunts, shuf-

fles about, stooped like an old man. Today I knew something bad had happened long before he opened his
mouth. The Germans shot 642 French villagers, among
them 190 schoolchildren, for aiding the enemy.

June 29 (GND): The Red Army has been driving back
the Germans for a week, breaking through their lines,
smashing their tanks.

July 6 (BND): Some more people on *our* side (Aunt
Lena's, Brother Martin's, *mine*) executed.

July 13 (GND): The Red Army continues to advance
on the Eastern Front.

July 20 (GND): Brother Martin was so excited he was
gasping for breath: "Hitler is d-dead. A b-bomb! Planted
by one of his own officers!"

July 21 (BND): Brother Martin's lips were hardly
moving when he said, "The evil man lives. The bomb
didn't kill him. The brave officer was shot." He raised
his eyes to the ceiling and whispered, "Help me understand thy ways, O God!"

I recited the poem I wrote about Slovakia to Brother
Martin. *Sunrise*, the weekly magazine read in all public
schools, never published it. The editor sent a note to my
teacher, Miss Sipková, asking why she doesn't choose a
poem by "one of our own." He knew by my family name
that I was Jewish.

Miss Sipková didn't tell me. She came to our house
with the note, to show Aunt Lena. She cried the whole
time, Aunt Lena said.

I bet Miss Sipková is on *our* side, too.

. . .

I kept my promise to surprise the Blessed Mother on Assumption Day.

For a shrine we chose the best picture I had of the Virgin, pasted it on a decorated cardboard box (we used crepe paper Marta saved from last year's Christmas present), and put it on a pedestal—the footstool little orphans use to reach the bathroom faucet. When Betka and I snuck corn kernels and beans out of storage for the rosaries, we also took two candles. Vlasta provided us with matches she slipped into her apron pocket while on kitchen duty.

In the afternoon I took three little girls to pick dandelions and any other pretty weeds we could find between the barn and the shed. The older girls wove them into garlands and strung them around the picture. Marta added beautiful flowers she made out of paper.

After lights-out I lit the two candles. We knelt at the little shrine and whispered fifty Hail Marys, keeping count with our corn-kernel rosaries. At the end we sang "Ave Maria" softly so the Sisters wouldn't hear in their rooms, but loud enough for the Blessed Mother to hear in heaven.

I can't help thinking about Brother Martin. If he knew what we were doing, August 15 would have been a very BND for him. Only this time I, not the war, would be to blame.

August 27 (GND): The German commander of Paris surrendered. General de Gaulle is walking in triumph through the city streets. The crowds are wild with cheering.

August 29 (GND): In the office a speech was blasting from a radio I had never seen before. Spread out on the table lay a large map of Slovakia. Only Sister Johanna and Brother Martin were there. Her face was white, his red.

A minute later the whole Krmanov staff rushed in to listen. There had been a Slovak National Uprising. Partisans had taken over the city of Banská Bystrica and declared a free Czechoslovak Republic. Brother Martin was pointing out on the map areas under their control. Some of the people in the room were smiling, some frowning.

When the speech finished, an orchestra started playing a melody. It sounded familiar, but I couldn't remember its name.

"Let's get all the children to the study, quickly." Brother Martin was already at the door. "Tell them what happened. It's time they knew who our true heroes are."

"Not so fast," Sister Johanna shouted at him. "Don't confuse the poor orphans. Your little revolt will be crushed in a few days."

He glared at her. "In a few days the partisans will be here, liberating us!"

Sister Mara spoke up. "Let's wait, Brother Martin, see what happens." He sighed.

Later I asked him about the familiar melody we heard on the radio. "It's the National Anthem of the Czechoslovak Republic," Brother Martin told me. "You don't remember?"

It is forbidden to sing or play that anthem in the independent Slovak State. The last time I heard it, I was four years old.

I often fantasize about Pavel. The basic plot, with variations each time, is this:

Pavel leads a troop of partisans (on horseback, on foot with banners) to battle. They fight (guns, swords, fists) the enemy—Germans and bad Slovaks (people I know—Sister Johanna, Rospačil, Andrej the chimney sweep—or only know of—President Tiso, his helpers Tuka, Mach, Vašek, etc.). Against all odds, the partisans win. We, the good Slovaks, cheer. Pavel lifts me off the ground, holds me up high as at the first time I met him, when my hair got tangled in the nut tree. Only this time I don't yell, "Put me down." I want everyone to see me in the arms of our hero. "This is my cousin Pavel," I shout for the whole world to hear. "Our liberator. My love."

September 5 (best GND ever): Saw Brother Martin bounding up the stairs three at a time. Radio Brussels announced that Germany surrendered.

September 6 (very BND): False announcement. Germany did not surrender.

Brother Martin is shrinking by the day, getting paler, while Sister Johanna, her cheeks burning bright red, expands.

German soldiers have overrun Slovakia and are trying to squelch the uprising.

I am worried sick about Pavel, and sad to see Brother Martin hurting so much.

. . .

Whenever Sister Johanna is in the office, Brother Martin keeps his mouth shut. He doesn't when Sister Mara is around. I think they listen to the forbidden radio broadcasts in secret, together.

When the armies on our side came to Normandy, Brother Martin said the war wouldn't last much longer. Now he says the same about the uprising. "They don't stand a chance," he told me. "It's their bodies against the German tanks."

"They're finished, Katarína, beaten. Those dear men and women, how bravely they fought." Brother Martin's voice is hoarse, his eyes red and swollen. "October 29 will mark a sad day in Slovak history. The partisan revolt is crushed." His eyes close. From under each lid a tear makes its way down his pale cheeks.

I am in the shed waiting for Sister Mara and Brother Martin. They have something important to tell me, she said.

Brother Martin looks around before he comes in to make sure no one is close enough to hear.

"Katarína," he starts, half-sitting on the handle of a rusty plow, "as you know, the Germans have occupied Slovakia. The Gestapo are looking for Jews everywhere, even in hospitals and orphanages. They've started deporting them again to camps outside the country . . ."

My stomach tightens. Will they tell me to leave, as Mariška Plčková did, because it's become too dangerous to keep me?

Sister Mara takes my trembling hand in hers. "Don't worry, Katarína, we'll make sure you are safe. Brother Martin and I are thinking of ways to hide you in case the Gestapo show up here. We'll let you know of our plan in the next few days."

I stay in the shed long after they're gone.

I love Sister Mara and Brother Martin. After Aunt Lena and Pavel I love them the most.

Everyone is jumping with joy. A rich lady invited all the orphans to town this Saturday to see a film, and after that for a treat in an ice cream parlor.

I am not jumping. Sister Johanna says I can't go to town, I mustn't show my face. "Mustn't show her face" was what Eva's mother said the time she didn't want me seen on their property. I told the Sister I'd bundle up with only my eyes and the tip of my nose showing, as I did then, but she said, "No, on Saturday you're to pretend to be sick."

This morning, while the girls shrieked with excitement and put on their Sunday clothes to go to town, I pretended I had a bellyache. I was so angry I actually did get one. But it turned out to be a wonderful day. I spent the afternoon helping Sister Mara in the laundry room. We pulled sheets through the mangle, stretched and folded them, and told each other stories.

The Sister tried to cheer me up. She said the film the children were seeing was about production of tires in the Northern Province. I didn't need cheering up; I was happy to have Sister Mara all to myself. She is young and pretty and blushes easily. She blushes a lot when Brother Martin is around. She said she might leave the Sisterhood after the war to start a family of her own.

I talked about Aunt Lena, Uncle Teo, and Anka. I said I didn't care much about Pavel, but Sister Mara guessed—she smiled and waggled her finger at me. I told her about the house, the noisy waiting room with chicken, duck, and goose heads popping out of bundles, the quacks, honks, and cackles driving Uncle Teo crazy. Sister Mara couldn't stop laughing. It got me started, too. I laughed until I couldn't stand up straight and tumbled into the stack of folded sheets. Brother Martin came down to find out what was so funny. We were laughing too hard to talk, so Brother Martin didn't find out, but he laughed anyway. No one felt like working anymore. At four o'clock the three of us sat at a small table, like a family, to snack on biscuits and stewed plums.

I wish the others were away every Saturday afternoon.

I've been counting the days till Christmas. "What presents did you get last year?" I asked Vlasta.

"The girls got new aprons," she said. "The boys got earmuffs."

I stopped counting.

Sister Mara saw me scratching my head. She sat me down on a stool and gave me another lice treatment.

This time no one pays attention to the red-nosed Turk in the yellow turban. Reeking of turpentine, I join the others at the long table to do homework.

Our heads pop up at the sound of strange voices and heavy footsteps coming down the hallway. The door opens. Two Germans in uniform are shown in by Brother Martin and Sister Mara. I go limp in my seat. Šebesta winks at me. In capital letters bold enough for me to see, he writes across his notebook: GESTAPO.

One of the Germans must be a high-ranking officer. In his polished boots, black leather gloves, and visored cap with the insignia of the Reich he looks as if he stepped off a magazine cover. My right hand slides into my pocket and grabs the rosary. With the other I pull the stinky yellow towel off my head and kick it under the table.

"Stand up, children."

Sister Mara's voice trembles, and her cheeks are whiter than her bonnet. She tells us to stand in two rows facing each other. The tall officer scans our faces, nods, slowly removes his gloves. Betka is the first in my row. I am next to the last.

"What is your name?"

He speaks Slovak with a heavy accent and sometimes doesn't understand the answer. The soldier at his side translates into German.

I am Katarína Zemanová, I keep telling myself between the Hail Marys, an orphan from Uhovce. But what I hear is Sister Johanna's voice, saying, "Truth won't hide behind a false name. It shows in everything—her speech, manners, expressions . . ."

"Where were you born?"

He is moving down between the two rows, coming closer. Brother Martin follows with a folder of documents, our birth certificates. The officer squints at the orphan he questions, then at the birth certificate, back and forth. He holds each document up against the light to see if the seal is forged. Soon he'll see that mine is.

"What is your religion? Why are you here?"

Three more children in my row, two in the other, then my turn. I am Protestant, I'll tell him. I am here because my parents are dead. What else will he ask? Will I know the right answer? "There is a lesson for you, Katarína," Sister Johanna's voice warns me. "One lie leads to another until you trip, and then God help you." Holy Mother, sweet Jesus, Patron Saint, guide me—

"What are *you* doing here, eh? Where is your Gypsy father?"

The officer is questioning dark-skinned Jožko. Brother Martin tries to answer for him but is silenced by a wave of the officer's black gloves.

"*Na ja*, where is he?"

Jožko bursts into tears. He swears that his father is not a Gypsy, that he is dead, that both his mother and father died before he was born.

Sister Mara turns red. Some of the big boys chuckle.

"*Ja*, so. No parents. You were dropped by a stork. But I can tell you are not a Gypsy. Gypsies make better liars."

I had better not lie. I'll trip and get Brother Martin and the Sisters into trouble. I'll say, look, Herr Officer, my birth certificate says I'm Protestant, but that's false. I am Catholic. I mean, I was born Jewish, but that doesn't count because Anka, our maid, saved me. Now Jesus wants me to help save these orphans—that's why I'm here. You can't be angry with Brother Martin and the Sisters, Herr Officer. They *had* to take me in. It was God's plan—

"Was is denn das? Was stinkt so?"

The officer, about to question the girl next to me, is crinkling his nose, sniffing, waving his gloves like a fan.

"That bad smell," the soldier translates. "The officer wants to know what it is. Where it's coming from."

Sister Mara steps forward. "It's this child"—she points at me—"an abandoned orphan they brought us from a village that—"

"Turpentine. That smell is turpentine," Brother Martin interrupts. "We're trying to rid her of lice."

"The officer might be smelling the ointment," Sister Mara says. "The child has scabies, a stubborn and very contagious strain we have in this region. I am using an ointment to—"

"Heraus mit ihr," the officer shouts even before the soldier finishes translating. *"Heraus!"*

"Get that child out of here!" the soldier commands.

Sister Mara hurries to obey. She grabs me by the wrist, pulls me from the lineup and out the door. At the end of the hallway she drops to her knees. "Thank you, God," she whispers, hugging me. "Thank you, oh, thank you!" Her cheeks feel wet and her shoulders tremble. She squeezes my hands, then abruptly stands up.

"Run to the shed, Katarína, and stay there until I send for you."

"Yes, Sister."

"And Katinka"—she calls me *Katinka*, as Aunt Lena does—"pray."

LIBERATED

We are watching bombers high overhead. They look bigger than the ones we usually see. Their sound, too, is different. Brother Martin thinks they might be American.

One of the bombers is flying lower, on a course of its own. Suddenly, fire shoots out of the plane. A dark bundle drops through the flames. The bomber plunges. A black trail follows it across the sky. The bundle opens into a large, white umbrella that floats in the sky.

Soon German army jeeps are roaring past the orphanage in the direction of the falling parachute. Soldiers with dogs pulling on leashes follow. I look up at the tiny man dangling in the sky. How frightened and lonely he must be.

"Hey, pilot!" I shout. "I'm happy you're alive. I am praying for you."

"Shut up," Brother Martin hisses. "He can't hear you. They, on the road, can."

He squeezes my shoulder and whispers, "I, too, am praying for the pilot. May the Lord be with him!"

. . .

I overheard Sister Mara and Brother Martin talking. Thousands of Slovak and Russian partisans died in the uprising.

Dear God, watch over Pavel. It's always freezing up in the mountains, and this is the coldest February in years. His ears must be all red and numb. If only I could be with him, I'd rub them till they tingled with warmth, I'd kiss the snowflakes off his eyelids, I'd make him tea with cinnamon and brandy.

Pavel is alive, I know he is.

Ever since the Gestapo came to Krmanov's looking for Gypsies and Jews, I've been wondering about God's plan. Does he really want me to save the Protestant orphans?

What would have happened if I didn't have lice and smell of turpentine? Or if Jožko's answer hadn't been so funny? What would they have done to Brother Martin and the Sisters if they'd caught them hiding us? I love Sister Mara and Brother Martin. They are the kind and brave people Aunt Lena talked about. Would God keep them out of heaven because they are Protestant? Or Aunt Lena, because she is Jewish?

I've been thinking about the rosary I dangle under the table while mouthing Protestant prayers, the picture cards I hide in my mattress, the stories of saints I tell the girls after lights-out. I am deceiving Brother Martin and the Sisters while they're taking a big risk to save me. Could God want that?

. . .

The Rabbi told Aunt Lena that no matter what she and I did or believed, we were Jewish and no one would let us forget it. I never understood what made me Jewish. It was like having some horrid deformity only others could see.

A few days before Christmas, Sister Mara asked me to come to the laundry room. She and Brother Martin were there, looking happy, smiling. On the ironing board was a row of candles, two eggs, a jar of honey, and a dish with walnuts and candy.

"It's Hanukkah," Sister Mara said. "Your holiday, Katarína. Brother Martin and I would like to learn about it and to celebrate with you."

"We know that Jews light candles," the Brother said, "but you'll have to tell us how many and what else we need besides the boiled eggs and the honey."

The Sister handed me matches. "Light the candles, Katarína. Let's hear you say a prayer or a blessing, in Hebrew."

I couldn't say a word. Not in any language. My chin quivered, the room spun, and the next thing I was sprawled on a heap of damp towels, sobbing. Only later did I begin to understand why.

The only religious holidays I ever celebrated, or wanted to, were Christian. Anything Jewish was ugly, shameful, like the big yellow star I was supposed to wear. When Sister Mara said that she and Brother Martin wanted to learn about Hanukkah and to celebrate it with me, the surprise was so big it made my knees buckle. And it started the tears.

The Brother and Sister thought I'd teach them how to celebrate the holiday. But I don't know any more than they do how many candles to light or what else is needed or the words to a single Hebrew prayer. I cried because I was ashamed of not being Jewish enough to know.

There were tears of happiness, too. To have taken all that trouble meant the Brother and Sister loved me as much as I loved them. More than anything, I wanted to return their happy smiles, but instead I was bawling on a heap of towels. I cried because I couldn't stop the crying.

That night Sister Mara wiped a few tears off her own face. She must have thought I was homesick, remembering Hanukkah celebrations with Aunt Lena.

The big yellow stars were like badges of shame all Jews were supposed to wear. The three elderly couples in my village wore them. So did my aunt and uncle. I refused to, and got away with it—almost.

A couple of weeks before I left to stay with the Plčkos, the two village policemen—one of them Škvorka, Božena's father—came to talk to Aunt Lena. I saw how difficult it was for her to tell me what she had to.

"Katinka," she said, "you were ordered to wear the Star of David. All this time you were supposed to wear it, Škvorka looked the other way—he said he wanted to spare you, a child, and the only Jewish child in this village. But he can't any longer. He has to answer to his superiors in the Hlinka Guard."

On the kitchen table lay a star. Not a small, pretty star with a blue border, like the ones Jews were ordered to wear at the time Aunt Lena and I left Bratislava. This was a large, ugly yellow patch.

"I won't wear that," I screamed. "I'm not Jewish. I don't want to be."

That evening Anka sewed a star on my coat.

Later that night I was in her room for more Catholic teachings. She told me about the Annunciation, one of the five Joyful Mysteries.

The next morning I walked out with my schoolbooks pressed tightly against my chest. With each step I felt that yellow blotch spreading, its six points, like tentacles, creeping out from under my books. I ripped the hateful thing off my coat, dug it with my heel into the ground, then prayed to my patron saint to keep the policemen from noticing.

I no longer think God sent me to Krmanov's to save the Protestant orphans. He must have sent me here to save me, from the Germans. When I told Brother Martin that I'd wanted to join the Hlinka Youth, he said, "Poor child, you were well taught what to think." Maybe I was well taught what to think about being Jewish, too. It might not be the horrid thing I've been made to feel it is. Aunt Lena said that after the war she'll teach me religion, *our* religion. I'll make sure she does. Lighting candles, eating candies, honey, and nuts sounds pretty good, and I suppose there are other holidays just as nice. I need to know what it is that everyone knows I am.

I stopped teaching the girls Catholic prayers. I pray to God, to Jesus, the Virgin, and my patron saint, but the rosary and the picture cards are buried outside the shed under a cross I marked on the wall.

The upper floor is closed. We orphans are living with the old people, on the ground floor. When the sirens start wailing, all of us rush to the basement.

We have to double up, one child and one old person in each bed. I sleep with Helen. She has a nice smell but can't stop shaking. It is her sickness. It makes the bed shake, and I have trouble falling asleep. Then, when I do, I wake up to Ratenica's crazy laughter.

The two Sisters have no time for us children. They tend the sick, the old, and now the wounded soldiers. The soldiers are ours; we hear them curse in Slovak while the Sisters dress their wounds. Evenings they play on their harmonicas, sad, slow tunes. Very different from the ones they sang and marched to at the start of the war.

Sitting in the basement gets boring. It's especially hard on the youngest orphans, the six-to-eight-year-olds. I had them draw faces on their fingers and name them. Now we're making up stories and plays, using our fingers as characters. Aunt Lena and I used to do that when I was little. We named the thumb Exordimus because he is so very important, strong, and independent. He is the only boy and a bit of a bully—the exact opposite of shy, clingy Princess Exilobí, the pinkie. The middle finger, Auntie Chalupka, was the head of the family and looked after the others, two on each side of her. We chose Atlonvévev for the ring finger, and for the finger that points, Aňaňaňa . . . I don't know why . . . Aunt Lena and I just kept making up silly sounds until we both cried from laughing so hard . . .

Yesterday we spent hours in the basement. They must have forgotten to sound the all-clear, I thought, as I waited for my chance to sneak upstairs to the orphanage.

I ran two flights up to the study, and through a rip in the blackout paper I watched soldiers walking along the dirt road on the hilltop above the cemetery. Troops have been shuffling past for the last few days. They look very tired; even their horses do. Brother Martin says they are a retreating contingent of the Hungarian army.

Suddenly there was a roar. Planes swooped down. They looked like winged monsters spilling black eggs from their bellies. The floor shook under my feet. Windows shattered. Through thick clouds of black smoke I could make out horses rearing and men scattering in all directions. The wounded horses writhed on the ground. Soldiers crumpled like puppets and rolled down the hill. I was too stunned to move.

At night I shook more than Helen. She says I screamed in my sleep.

Today I am back upstairs, looking out at the cemetery. I see bodies sprawled over graves, slumped over tombstones. Some of the wounded soldiers were brought to Krmanov's Home of Love; some crawled here on their own. Now the curses and prayers we hear are in Slovak and in Hungarian.

Whoever can, helps. Old people who for years had done nothing but eat and sleep are cooking, cleaning, and washing and have new strength to order us orphans about.

Brother Martin teaches us when he can, once or twice a week. We carry food to the wounded soldiers, spoonfeed them, sponge their foreheads, sweep, mop, empty slop pails. The Slovak soldiers ask us to read them old letters from home. Peter can read but has bandages over his eyes. He might never see again.

"Is it you, Katarína?"

"Yes, Peter."

"Read me the letter, will you?"

I open it carefully—it's so worn at the folds I'm afraid it will fall apart in my hands.

" 'Dear son, when are you coming home . . . ?' "

Peter knows the letter by heart. So do I. It's four pages long, but I rarely get to read much before Kača shrieks from the kitchen, "Katarína, where are you? There's work to do. Get back here at once."

Old Kača has turned into a general. She plans, organizes, commands. Evenings we watch Ratenica mimic her. She also mimics the Sisters and some other old people—Uncle Hrnec, Cross-eyed Cupek, Mad Magdaléna.

Magdaléna paints her face and sings Gypsy songs. Old Hrnec beats rhythms on a rusty pot. Only for Samuel the world hasn't changed. He still sits by the door, tense, like a tightly wound spring about to snap.

The Hungarian soldiers are gone. The language we hear now, besides Slovak, is German.

Brother Martin is quietly cursing the German commandant for positioning their artillery in our yard. It turned us into a target, he said.

When the first German soldiers appeared, I thought that I should hide, but Sister Mara said, "No need. They're too busy trying to save their own skins to worry about you."

One of them, Otto, likes to rock me on his knee. He says I remind him of his daughter, Ingelein. She, too, has red hair and freckles.

I should hate Otto, but he looks so tired, not at all like the elegant officer who came here looking for Jewish and Gypsy children. I pray for the Russians and Americans to kill all our enemies, but I also pray for Otto to get back to Ingelein.

What I dreaded would happen finally did. Without any warning, Samuel pounced at Mad Magdaléna and started to choke her.

It took five men to hold him down. Samuel howled, kicked, and flailed his arms at some monster only he could see. His wild green eyes blazed with a light so strong I had to close mine.

Sister Johanna injected him in the arm. Soon after, Samuel lay on the floor, sucking his thumb. I feel sad. If only someone could make him see that there is no monster attacking him. But would that make him hear things *not* in his head? The sirens? Would he then cower in the basement like the rest of us, waiting for bombs to explode?

Brother Martin is bounding up the steps two at a time, whistling the old Czechoslovak anthem. I run after him.

"Brother Martin, don't. Someone might hear you."

He turns around, smiles.

"You're in a good mood. Why?"

He winks at me, tousles my hair. "It's the first day of spring, Katarína, don't you know?"

The sounds of cannon and artillery grow fainter each day. We had our first civilian visitor in weeks—Vlasta's aunt. All of us surrounded her, asking for news. She looked about as if to make sure no enemy was listening, then whispered, "They're coming. We can see, from our village. They'll be here any day now." Brother Martin threw his arms around her, then started whistling the anthem again. Right there, in front of everybody.

·　　·　　·

"Whistling the Czechoslovak anthem. Someone should report him."

We are in the storage room, getting potatoes and turnips for supper.

"Why don't you, Šebesta? Your uncle is in the Hlinka Guard."

"His uncle must be shitting in his pants. When the Russians get here, he and his buddies will be swinging from trees."

"Shut your mouth, you Gypsy turd. It's you were shitting in your pants when the Gestapo were here."

Emil gets between Jožko and Šebesta to keep them apart. The rest of us keep filling our baskets. The potatoes feel like hard snowballs. My fingers are numb from the cold.

"Why would Brother Martin want the Germans to lose the war?" asks Vlasta. "They're on our side."

"The good Slovaks want the Russians to win," Jožko tells her. "The collaborators, like Šebesta's uncle, are German ass-lickers."

Šebesta flings a potato at Jožko. Jožko makes donkey ears at Šebesta.

"Are you saying that the Hlinka Guards and our President, even, are bad Slovaks?"

I, too, used to wonder about that. I'd come home from Hlinka Youth meetings—the three or four I went to— beaming with pride only to find Aunt Lena annoyed by my patriotic chatter. That's why I never invited any of my Hlinka Youth sisters home. I worried that Aunt

Lena's feelings about our Slovak heroes would show on her face.

"The Russians are Slavs, like us. It's not natural that we should fight them."

Emil scores a point. Family means a great deal in an orphanage. But not to Šebesta.

"You just wait till those Antichrist Bolsheviks get here. They'll tear your nails out at the mention of Jesus."

Betka cringes, hides her hands in her pockets. "What about the Hungarians? They're not family."

"Them? They change sides when the tide turns."

"Not the Hungarians, cabbage-head! The Italians. They're the traitors."

"Don't listen to him, he's got straw between his ears. It's the Romanians that change sides."

Betka sighs. "All those armies. Maybe they just get mixed up and forget who they're fighting."

Emil lifts her off the ground. "That must be it. Three cheers for Betka, the wisest orphan in Krmanov's Home of Love."

"Let's get these turnips to the kitchen," Vlasta reminds us, "or we'll have Kača after us."

Too late. Here comes Kača, grumbling, shaking her fist.

The German artillery is long gone from our yard. Ambulances have taken away the wounded. Yet we find ourselves walking on tiptoe through the long, empty halls and talking in whispers. Something is about to happen.

Brother Martin and the Sisters often stop whatever they're doing and listen. Two or three times a day they climb the hill above the cemetery to scan the horizon.

"Get up, everybody, come look, they're here!"

We jump out of our beds and follow Brother Martin up the steps to the orphanage study.

"We don't need this anymore," he says, tearing the blackout paper off the windows. "Let's have light."

Is it a wedding party, that lively column on the road above the cemetery? Men in fur hats and flared, belted shirts bounce in carts, waving red banners. Horses, three to a cart, trot at a brisk pace. Brother Martin pushes open the windows. We hear singing. Men's voices. Harness bells. But where are the women, I wonder, and why are there no children?

"Where is the bride, Brother Martin? How come she isn't here?"

"She is." He laughs, lifting me in his arms. "Slovakia is the bride. She is liberated. Our brothers, the Russians, are here!"

Krmanov's Home of Love is filled with Russian soldiers. There is singing and laughter all day long and late into the night. Even those hobbling on crutches are cheerful.

Betka and the other little orphans haven't touched ground for days—they are passed from arms to arms. At times a soldier will try to embrace Sister Mara, and then Brother Martin shakes his finger and shouts, "No vodka for you, no more vodka." They all want vodka. I heard the cook complain that she has to keep everything that contains alcohol under lock and key. Even furniture polish.

The soldiers spend all their time with us orphans. They tell us jokes and stories in Russian. We don't understand, but love to listen. Their language sounds like bird chatter. They teach us songs, do magic tricks, play on balalaikas, clown, dance. But nothing makes them happier than giving us presents. We get candy, foreign coins, stamps, picture postcards, pens, pencils, and still the soldiers turn their pockets inside out to find more things to give us.

Vlasta jealously guards a worn shaving brush. Jožko flaunts a rusty key. Šebesta likes the Russians now; he shows off his collection of gun shells. I treasure my picture of Uncle Stalin.

When I go to bed, I put his picture on my pillow. I kiss his bushy mustache, then snuggle against him, cheek to cheek, as I fall asleep.

We cried to see the Russians leave. Now there are Romanian soldiers about, but we have little to do with them. They sit in tight circles on the stone floors playing cards, and give us suspicious looks when we pass by. We stay out of their way.

We've moved back upstairs, to the orphanage. I'm happy to have a bed to myself.

The talk after lights-out has turned to boys. The older girls have nothing else on their minds.

Vlasta swoons over Emil. Marta sighs over Šebesta, the bed-wetter. Poor Šebesta. He no longer pees in his bed, but the boys still tease him about his sheet being wet most mornings. When I say that makes no sense, they chuckle and make faces at each other.

Jožko is funny, but I can't get excited about anyone in short pants. I love Pavel.

Someday Pavel will make me a maypole that will tower above all the others in the village. That night I won't sleep a wink: I'll be listening for his footsteps on the roof, for the sounds of tapping and scraping in our chimney. Then, the morning of the First of May, those long, colored ribbons and streamers will swirl in the breeze for everyone to see. "Look at that maypole," they'll say. "It's Katarína's. Pavel must love her. He must love her very much . . ."

We're back to routine: classes, chores, prayers. I keep asking Brother Martin, "Is the war over? Can I go home? Are they still looking for Jews?"

No, he says, the war isn't over yet, but they won't be looking for Jews in our orphanage. This part of the country has been liberated.

"Was my village liberated?"

"Yes. Before we were."

"Then why can't I go home?"

"Be patient, child. There is no civilian transportation,

but we'll find a way. And, Katarína," he adds, "you needn't lie to the children anymore. You can tell them you're Jewish."

Great news to tell my Catholic converts. I think I'll wait a while.

At night I hear Marta, in the bed next to mine, whispering prayers to the Holy Virgin.

There are no buses or cars in sight, only army jeeps, yet I watch the road. The phone lines are dead, but I listen for the phone to ring. Mail hasn't come in weeks, still I expect a letter from Aunt Lena. And every night I dream of home.

Last night I dreamed I was onstage and had to dance to music everyone heard but me. It reminded me of what happened the day my school performed a play in the village Culture House.

Our teacher, Miss Sipková, gave me the part of a Dancing Orchid. I was to prepare the dance steps and choose the music. I chose the "Blue Danube Waltz" from Uncle Teo's record collection.

The afternoon performance started out well. I was waiting in the wings, taking peeks to find Aunt Lena in the audience, when Miss Sipková came up, crying, "Katarína, you can't dance. The priest sat on the 'Blue Danube.' It split in two. We're stopping the play."

"But why?" I argued. "Put on another record."

"It's too late. There's no time to learn new steps—"

I didn't listen. I never learn any steps in advance, I just

move to the music. I raced to the storeroom and out of a dusty bin pulled the first record I touched. Next thing, I was onstage, dancing.

I didn't think I did well, the music was boring, but Miss Sipková was pleased. "We're lucky," she said. "Most records in that bin are drills. You might have had to dance to a multiplication table or a spelling list."

Before the evening performance I set out to find the "Blue Danube"—there were five other families in the village with Victrolas. I was lucky again.

That evening I danced well. Pavel was in the audience.

I wondered whether, in my long, white dress, I looked like the woman I'd be in ten years when I'd be old enough to marry him.

I am in Sister Mara's room, for a talk. When she asked me to come she wasn't smiling. I was sure it would be about the bathtub I forgot to clean. The last time it happened I promised never to forget again.

The Sister makes me sit at the table while she paces the floor. I am about to offer to do extra chores on Saturday when she pulls up a chair and starts talking.

"Katarína, I have something important to tell you. Listen carefully."

I squirm in my chair.

"We know how eager you are to go home and we heard from—"

"Aunt Lena—you heard from her! Is she coming?"

"Calm down, child. Your aunt wouldn't be able to get

here. There might not be any civilian transportation for weeks."

I slump in my chair. What good is this liberation if there is no way to go home or hear from home?

Sister Mara takes a large white handkerchief out of her pocket and dabs at the tears I am not able to hold back.

"I asked you to my room to tell you about Sergiu. You know, that nice Romanian officer staying with us. Brother Martin spoke to him about you. There's a chance you can go home with an army convoy."

"When? What's a convoy?"

"Two trucks and a command car will be leaving to check on soldiers in hospitals. We heard from Sergiu that they'll be passing close to your village, and Brother Martin asked—"

"When, Sister! When are they leaving?"

She smiles. "As soon as he gets the trucks. He thinks the day after tomorrow."

The walls are rippling, I am hugging Sister Mara, we are both laughing. But suddenly her mood changes.

"Katarína, there is something you need to prepare yourself for, with God's help."

She stops talking. When she continues, her voice is so low I have to lean forward.

"It's possible, Katinka, that when you get home your Aunt Lena won't be there."

"But she *is*! My village was liberated before we were,

Brother Martin told me. She's home with Uncle Teo. Pavel, too. And Anka. Everybody's back."

"I pray for that, Katarína, but we can't always understand God's ways. You, too, need to pray, ask him for strength and guidance . . ."

I want to run out of the room, to tell the girls. The boys, too. And the old people. Helen, Kača, cross-eyed Cupek, old Hrnec. I must remember to leave a note for Olga, with my address. There's so much to do. Presents! I have nothing to bring home. I'll ask the girls to help me make some . . . And I need to get my things ready, polish the black shoes, iron my good dress. The rosary! The rosary and the holy picture cards buried outside the shed—

"Are you listening, Katarína? The officer will be returning to us, here. If it's God's will—I mean, if need be, he'll bring you back—"

"I'll wait there. I can stay with Miss Sipková, my teacher—but I won't need to. They're all home, waiting for *me*!"

Sister Mara sighs, then takes my hand. "All right, Katinka. Just know that Brother Martin and I love you. You'll always have a home here with us."

Only then does it occur to me, it's goodbye to her, too. To Sister Mara and this cozy little room where she brought me that first day when I fainted in the study. It was on this bed that I awoke to find her watching over me. After tomorrow I won't see her face or hear her laugh. I can't stand the thought of it.

"I love you, Sister Mara. I'll come back to visit, with Aunt Lena, the minute school lets out."

She wipes her eyes. "Here, Katarína, take back your monkey puppet."

I reach out for Stefie—then let my hand drop. "Sister, the children have no toys. I'll leave this one for them as a remembrance."

"That's generous, but with all those little fingers grabbing for it, the puppet wouldn't last a week. Take it. You'd miss it. The two of you shared some bad times."

Sister Mara is right. I missed Stefie the minute I made my hasty offer.

"We need to get you ready. Woolen socks, gloves, boots. It'll be cold in the mountains."

I feel impatient again. I long to see mountains and rivers. My river, Orava. It will be wild and swollen with all the ice melted. And the pussy willows along the banks will be sprouting their fuzzy gray blooms.

"May I go now, Sister?" She nods.

I race out the door. Up to the study, down to the old-age home, out to the shed, the basement, the laundry room, back to the study, and all the time I keep telling myself—it's not a dream, it's true. I am leaving the orphanage, I am going home!

ORAVA, MY RIVER

This morning, just a couple of days over a year since I came, I left Krmanov's Home of Love.

We are spending the night in an army camp. I think the officers are angry with Sergiu for bringing me. There was shouting in Romanian, and from the looks I got I could tell it was about me. I worry that they'll make him take me back to the orphanage.

The room where they put me up for the night must be the camp infirmary. Everything is clean and white and smells of iodine. It reminds me of the girls' dormitory at the orphanage, of how I felt about it when I first came to Krmanov's Home of Love. Rows of white beds lined up against white walls, no pictures, books, or toys. It's like a ward in a hospital, I thought then. But this morning, waving goodbye, I felt I was leaving a warm, friendly place. I wondered about the new orphan that would be assigned to my bed, and I didn't like the idea. It was *my* bed!

I am tired. We rode for many hours on bumpy roads.

At checkpoints Sergiu shouts, flaunts papers, and gets us through ahead of everyone else. Our convoy is small, a command car and two trucks. I ride with Uncle Sergiu— that's what he asked me to call him—in the command car. The trucks follow.

Sergiu shouts in Romanian at our driver, Niku. To me he speaks softly, in Slovak. He knows many words, but they come out in the wrong order, like, "Sleeping will you now?" To make sure I understand he acts out his questions in pantomime—chews on a bite of air, drinks from an imagined flask. When I need to pee, I tug at Sergiu's sleeve, he signals our driver, the driver stops at the nearest bush. Sometimes it takes a while before we see one. Flat, empty fields stretch on both sides of the road. Boring. I could hardly keep my eyes open today.

I bet the girls at the orphanage couldn't, either. We stayed up last night making plans. Vlasta, Betka, and Marta will be coming to our house for Christmas every year. Olga, too, if she can. All seventeen girls will be coming during school vacations with Sister Mara, starting this summer. Seventeen! How will we find space for them? Aunt Lena will—she'll want to. But Uncle Teo? In all the excitement, I forgot about him. He isn't going to like the idea.

Someone's coming. It's Sergiu, with a blanket under his arm.

"Here." He hands it to me. "You open blanket."

Rolled inside is a small package wrapped in newspaper.

"Look," he tells me. "I think very much you like it."

When I see what Sergiu brought, I want to throw my arms around him.

"Oh, yes, Uncle Sergiu, thank you! Very, very much I like it."

I haven't seen, smelled, or tasted chocolate in nearly two years. The last time I did was a bar Pavel left for me under my pillow.

We're halfway home—Sergiu showed me, on a map. The distance we traveled in two days fits between my middle finger and thumb, same as the distance that's still ahead. In only two more days I'll be home!

We are staying at an inn that had a large sign saying NO ROOMS. Sergiu paid no attention to the sign. There was whispering, things were passed under the table, and now we have a large room with soft beds and fluffy down pillows. For supper we had roast goose while people at other tables were served boiled potatoes with cabbage. I hugged my plate close to me to ward off the evil eye.

Sergiu is never tired. In the towns he often disappears, then comes back with treats—slivovitz and cigarettes for the men, sweets for me. He doesn't say what he gets for himself, but I see that he is wearing a different watch today.

I don't like being left with our driver, Niku. He keeps staring at me. Yesterday he pinched my cheek; today, my leg. Fat, clammy fingers with hair growing on them. I won't tell Sergiu; he might decide it was a bad idea to take me along.

The other four soldiers, from the trucks, keep to themselves. When we stop to eat or to rest, Niku walks over to sit with them. They talk low but laugh loud. Telling dirty jokes, I bet.

At noon we stopped at the roadside to eat. Sergiu showed me a picture of his daughter, Klara. She is five. Dark, curly hair, lively black eyes, like Sergiu's. "Pretty," I said. "You must miss her a lot." He nodded. Then he asked, "You in orphanage happy? The Sisters good to you?" I told him that Sister Mara and all the girls were coming to my house for the summer. "So," he said. "Big surprise for you family, eh?"

At this time, I was thinking, the girls at Krmanov's are lining up for their Tuesday meal—a ladleful of squash. I used to hate Tuesdays because they were squash days. Today I am chewing on a tasty sausage with Sergiu, and next Tuesday I'll be gobbling up apricot dumplings with poppy seeds and sugar because that's what I'll ask Aunt Lena to make every day, forever.

Tonight, for supper at the inn, I wore the pretty dress Sister Mara gave me. I told her thank you, no, I have lots of dresses at home, but she reminded me: those won't fit anymore.

Pavel will be back from the mountains. Will he notice how I've grown? Will he be watching me now, when he thinks no one is looking, the way he used to watch Anka?

Pavel, only two more days before I see you!

. . .

I won't be seeing Pavel in two days. We're creeping like turtles.

The countryside is no longer flat, it looks like home—mountains, forests, castles carved into high cliffs with wild rivers churning below. I feel my heart racing and can hardly stop myself from shouting, faster, faster! Instead, we stop. Another blown-up tunnel. Another blown-up bridge. More waiting. More walking.

Our convoy broke up. Niku drove Sergiu and me as far as the river and turned back to the army camp. Good riddance, I thought. A few hours earlier, when Sergiu left us alone, that stinker pinched my behind. Sergiu came back wearing two new watches.

What's left of the bridge ahead of us looks like a monster with a slit belly, its entrails spilling out, dangling over the water. The raft can take across only a few people at a time, and there are lots of us waiting—Russian and Slovak soldiers, laborers, men with briefcases in Sunday suits, peasants in colorful embroidered costumes, and animals. Besides the chickens, geese, and ducks peeking out of bundles I see a calf, a colt, three goats, and two pigs.

Sergiu isn't his usual self, or else we'd long be on the other side of the river. Maybe he doesn't dare to shout and barter in front of the Russian soldiers. I noticed that he took off both his watches. "Beautiful," he keeps saying, pointing at the snow-capped mountains. "Like home. Like Romania." Earlier he caught me sniffing the chocolate. His eyes grew wide. "You not eat? No like?" I told him I was saving it for Aunt Lena; she'll need it for the cake she'll be baking for my eleventh birthday. He walked away, shaking his head, to sit by himself on a rock, by the river.

Each time the raft gets back, everyone pushes to get on, but Sergiu doesn't move. He must be homesick, sad to be so far from his family.

Yesterday, after we crossed the river, Sergiu hired Matej, a shepherd, to show us shortcuts over the mountains. We were climbing up a rocky path when sirens started blasting in the towns below. We wondered what happened. When it started getting dark, Matej took us into his hut for the night. We slept on the earthen floor with only sheepskins for covers. This morning I ache all over.

It's dark in here. The only light comes from an opening in the ceiling. A circle of blue. It must be late morning, but there is no sign of Matej or Sergiu. How are we going to get home—hike all the way? I'll outgrow my new dress before we get there!

This mug of milk, smoked cheese, and black bread on the floor must be my breakfast. Same as last night's supper. Before I met Pavel, I used to daydream about being married to a shepherd—making music together on *fujaras*, flutes we carved out of wood, playing hide-and-seek in the meadows, huddling by campfires under the stars, saying love poems to each other. I never thought of sleeping on an earthen floor or eating the same meal twice every day. I also never imagined my shepherd to look like Matej—tall, stooped, with buck teeth and stringy hair. Or to smell like him. Forget poetry. He hardly talks. He grunts.

Where is Sergiu? What's keeping him? My birthday is in eight days—we'll never make it home in time. If he doesn't get here by the time I count to—um—twenty, I'll start running and won't stop until I hear our squeaky garden gate.

Before I start on the counting, I take a look outside. There is Sergiu, coming up the path. He bounces with every step as if he had springs in his shoes. The minute he sees me, Sergiu shouts, "Germany surrender! That why siren yesterday. No more war in Europe. Finish."

I run into his open arms.

Sergiu has left me on a farm for two days while he visits Romanian soldiers in a hospital. That, he reminded me, was the reason he was sent on this trip, so I held back the tears.

The farm belongs to Ján Hulák and his wife. His mother and five brothers and sisters live with him. They call the mother old Huláčka and the wife young Huláčka.

It is a strange-looking farmhouse, not like the ones I remember from my village. This one is built out of bricks, like houses in town, but it doesn't have a bathroom. Young Huláčka told me to use the outhouse during the day but at night not to bother going that far. "Go anywhere along the fence," she said.

The rooms, too, look different. No crucifix, no pictures of saints, no little shrines. Instead, there are faces of men with mustaches and beards and signs in large letters saying: WORKERS OF THE WORLD, UNITE! RELIGION IS THE OPI-something OF THE PEOPLE! And another sign, about people losing their chains.

This morning after Sergiu left and, I thought, everyone else, too, I wandered about the farm. When I opened the door to one of the sheds, someone shrieked. It was old Huláčka, kneeling in front of a picture of the Virgin, clutching a rosary. She was happy to see it was only me. She said that her children used to be devout Catholics but are now Communists and won't let her go to church or pray. "I do it in secret," she said. "See?" She turned over the picture of the Virgin. On the other side was the face I saw hanging over Ján Hulák's bed. "Karl Marx," she said. Must be someone in their family, I thought, though he doesn't look like a peasant. Maybe an uncle in America. I told her that when I was in the Protestant orphanage, I, too, used to pray to the Virgin Mary in secret. Only I never thought of putting her picture in back of Martin Luther's!

At supper the young people talked about their work. Ján Hulák, slurping his potato soup, turned to me. He wanted to know about my family, what kind of work Uncle Teo did. I told him. He frowned. When I mentioned Anka, he asked, "Who is she, your sister?"

"No," I said, "our maid. She is back, too."

His fist hit the table so hard the tin bowls jumped.

"No she isn't!" he shouted. "You will have to sweep your own room, little Countess, and your aunt will have to bake her own bread!"

She always does, I thought, but I was too scared to talk back to him.

Later that night old Huláčka came to the room I share with Sergiu. She told me that Ján wanted me out of his house.

"I can't leave," I whimpered. "I need to wait for Uncle Sergiu. Is it because I am Jewish?"

"No, my pigeon. It's because of Anka. About her being your maid. He says you think like a capitalist."

A *what?*

"Don't mind him, little one. I'll keep you fed and comfortable until the officer gets here."

Hurry, Sergiu. Hurry back.

Sergiu came back in two days, just as he promised. When I told him that Ján Hulák wanted us out of his house because I think like a capitalist, Sergiu laughed so hard he had to lean on a chair to keep his balance.

We had a festive supper—venison with potato dumplings and sweet red cabbage. Ján Hulák kept staring at his new watch and filling his glass with beer. He often smiled at me. "Stay in my home as long as you like," he said. I was happy to hear Sergiu answer, "Thank you, but leave must we in morning." Ján invited Sergiu to play cards with him and his brothers after supper. He said that in the morning he'd give us a ride to the nearest town.

. . .

I wake up when Sergiu comes to our room. "Uncle Sergiu, have you heard about Karl Marx? Is he famous?"

"Yes. Marx very much famous."

"Why? What did he do?"

Sergiu pulls a chair over to my bed. "Marx don't do. He think. Think very much. He dead now. Live before hundred years."

"Is he a Slovak hero?"

"Not Slovak. Born in Germany. He and friend, Engels, invent Communism. They say, Down with capitalist. Workers throw over the rich, everybody own means of produce . . ."

I don't learn anything more because my eyes won't stay open. I fall asleep.

"Sergiu, look at the storks nesting on that chimney!"

I'm glad we're traveling again. This morning, Ján Hulák drove us to the nearest town. I like it. Children are riding new, shiny bikes, calling to one another; birds chatter in the chestnut trees. The small houses look as if they are freshly painted, the little gardens in front are pretty, white lace curtains show off orange, pink, and purple geraniums blooming in window boxes.

We turn a corner and suddenly there is a street like no other—broken windows, doors boarded up with Stars of David painted on them. There are no people, no sounds, only some skinny cats prowling in overturned garbage cans. The signs above empty shops have Hebrew letters on them.

"Uncle Sergiu, Jews must have lived here."

He grabs me by my coat sleeve and starts walking away so fast I have to run to keep up.

"Why aren't they back? This town is liberated, isn't it?"

"They not back yet. They not in a hurry, like you."

"Are they still in those work camps, you think?"

He shrugs.

"How long will they have to stay there? The war's over, why can't they come home?"

"I don't know," he shouts. "Now be quiet. You make me crazy!"

We are back on the street with the freshly painted houses, but I am seeing empty ones with broken windows, boarded-up doors. Where are the people who lived there? What happened to them? "Deported to Poland." "In a labor camp here, in Slovakia." "Shot." "Rotting in the county jail." Voices from Klietky, villagers arguing about "that couple caught two months ago." I start running, same as then, can't see a thing for the tears, bump my head against a wall. I kick it, pound it with my fists. "Why can't they leave the Jews alone? Why? What did we do?"

Sergiu squeezes my shoulder. He keeps his hand on my shoulder the whole time I'm crying.

At night I find a note on my pillow. It says: SORRY I SHOUTED YOU.

We've been waiting for ferries, walking over mountains, sitting at inns, and riding on whatever Sergiu manages to arrange. This time it's a wagon pulled by oxen. There is nothing slower. I'd rather walk. I feel so impatient Sergiu has to keep me from jumping off.

Another river. Another blown-up bridge. The farmer turns the oxen around and throws down our bundles.

"You wait here for the ferry," he tells us. "It comes by a few times a day."

No one else is waiting. Sergiu sits down on a log and studies the map. "Hmmmm," he mumbles. "This river called Orava."

It stops my breath. "Uncle Sergiu, did you say Orava?" He nods. The next thing, my arms are around his neck and I am shouting, "Orava, my river, I am home!"

I dip my hands into the cold water. These little waves passing between my fingers flowed through my village. Through Eva's village, too. She might have seen that branch tossing in the water. Maybe Božena or Karla or Terka was at the river and reached for it—they are always looking out for sticks to shoo the geese.

"Uncle Sergiu, look how fast that branch is going. I wish we could make ourselves small, like in a fairy tale, and ride on it."

"We don't get there. The river go wrong way. The way we going, we get there."

"When, Uncle Sergiu? When?"

"Soon. We close." He shows me on the map. The distance between where we are and home is the width of Sergiu's thumb.

"What is that big mountain there? Does it say on the

map?" When he tells me, I feel dizzy. "Uncle Sergiu, my village is in the valley right behind that mountain. We see it from our kitchen window. Aunt Lena might be looking at it right now."

He picks up a large stone and throws it into the river. I look for a round, flat one and try to make it skip. It does. One, two, three, four times! I'll challenge Pavel to a stone-skipping contest.

It's raining. We are staying in a guesthouse, in two rooms for the price of one. Sergiu knocked on my door before, for breakfast. I told him I had a stomachache, which wasn't true. I am angry. Last night he said we wouldn't travel today if it rained. How stupid!

Strange—it's Sunday, but I don't hear any church bells. Anka would be in church now and Pavel sleeping—he never gets up Sundays before noon. And Aunt Lena—oh, if only she knew that in two more days I'll be home, and the day after that we'll be celebrating my birthday together! If not for the stupid rain I'd be home tomorrow—on the map we are closer than the width of my little finger.

It had better not rain much this summer. I want to show Sister Mara and the girls the Witches' Pool, take them berry-picking, ride with them on a raft down the Orava River, to the old castle. Poor Vlasta, Betka, they don't get to go outdoors for fun, just to do chores in the yard or to help with the shopping. This morning they are downstairs, singing hymns, with the old people . . . Kača shrieking, old Hrnec croaking like a frog, Mad Magdaléna singing tunes of her own . . . every time I think about it I laugh, but now I am crying. Is it because of the rain? Because of my dream last night?

In the dream I kept coming closer to our house and at the same time getting farther away. Aunt Lena was standing at the window, but then, suddenly, her face would turn into a different one—the face of Sister Johanna. What was *she* doing in our house? And why was there a spiked iron fence? Our house has a green gate with lilac bushes around it!

Just thinking about that dream is giving me a stomachache. Now I don't have to feel bad about having lied to Sergiu.

"Here we rest."

"Here? Why, we can rest at home. You can see my house from that hill, I'll show you."

"We stay in this village tonight. We here sleep."

"Uncle Sergiu, look at the map. See how close we are? You can't fit a poppy seed between this village and mine."

"We don't come like this. Tired, dusty. Enough walking today."

"Listen, Uncle Sergiu, I know exactly where we are. This is where my aunt and uncle and I were hiding, in a barn. We're one hour's walk from home."

"Tomorrow morning is better."

"Sergiu—"

"Be quiet now. We stay tonight here."

I cried, begged, called him names. He dragged me, howling, to the nearest inn. I wouldn't go to supper with him; he went by himself. And he locked my door because I said I knew my way home and no one could keep me away!

How lucky that the window faces the fields: he won't see me jump. And if he comes after me, he won't find me. I won't be on the road. I'll climb that hill, run down the other side, and be home in half the time.

The bundle can stay—Anka and I will pick it up some other time. Or Sergiu will bring it tomorrow. I'll carry only the chocolate, in my coat pocket, and, in the other pocket, Stefie. I won't leave her behind. A note for Sergiu? No. He'll see the open window, he'll understand.

Hmmmm—*down* wasn't so far away when I looked out before. But I can do it, I've jumped from higher places in Karla's barn, in Uncle Dodák's orchard. All right, then: one, two, three—jump! Ouch, my ankle. That stupid rock, I didn't see it. No wonder. There's no moon. Only a few stars and black clouds. But I'll find my way. The village lights will be behind me, they'll help on this side of the hill, and once I'm over the crest I won't need to worry: there'll be lots of lights shining up at me from my own village just below.

A footpath. This one. No, that one. It doesn't matter, I know where I need to go—to the top. And what I must watch out for—rocks. Puddles. Cow dung. Thistles. I wish the moon were full, the way it was when I snuck out to the Witches' Pool. How scared I was that night. And how silly. As if only my freckles kept Pavel from falling in love with me. Me, a scrawny fourth-grader.

Sergiu didn't laugh when I told him how Old Krasovka tricked me; today all my chatter went right past his ears. "You not must go back to orphanage," he kept mumbling. "Romania good country. You be big sister to Klara."

I'd like that . . . a little sister to play with, seeing Sergiu again . . . I'll ask Aunt Lena to let me visit them next summer . . . I hope he'll still want me to . . . I shouted at him, called him bad names, and now I'm running away . . . But I know he'll forgive me. He'll come tomorrow, he'll be with us to celebrate my birthday . . .

Aunt Lena and I will bring in armfuls of lilacs from the garden . . . and then I'll surprise her with the chocolate and she'll bake my favorite cake . . . Pavel will be there, Anka, Uncle Teo . . . Božena . . . she won't be angry anymore, she'll understand why I couldn't tell her my secret . . . and Eva, too . . . this time her mother will let her come, the war's over—

Ouch! Another stupid rock. And on my aching foot, too. Now it hurts so much I can hardly walk. I can't see a step ahead; even the stars are gone. Those black clouds mean rain. Oh, please, God, not before I get home. And no thunder, either. It scares me.

This hill is steeper than it looked. And higher. But I'm getting close. Only a bit more and I'll be looking down at my house! The thought of it gives me goose bumps. No one at home knows how close I am, how soon I'll be with them. I wonder what they're doing—sitting at the table after supper, talking?

No! Today is Tuesday, Aunt Lena and Anka are making dough, for bread. Aunt Lena's hair is covered with her blue kerchief, Anka's is pulled back in a tight braid . . . They're bending over the big blue basin, sifting flour, crushing boiled potatoes . . . At first they don't hear the knock on the door but then, knock—knock again, they look up, look at each other, wonder . . . Anka comes to the door, squints into the darkness . . . Who is this girl, what does she want? Could it be . . . ? No, this girl's too grown, it can't be . . . But Anka steps closer, looks again, her eyes grow wide, and—Ježiš Mária, it is! Holy saints, it's she, she's here, Katarínka is back!

It can't be more than eight steps to the top. Ten at the most. Six . . . five . . . four . . . three . . . At last! I made it!

Below is my village. It must be. But there are no lights! There are no lights anywhere in the valley except the ones behind me, where I came from.

How can that be? Come here, Stefie. Look! Did we get lost in the dark? Climb the wrong hill? I must have been wrong about the time: it's late, much later than I thought. Everyone in the village has gone to bed. Oh, there—I think I see a light—one! Over by the bakery. It must be Tomáš staying up, baking bread.

I can't walk anymore, Stefie, my ankle's hurting worse. Do we roll down? If we did, we'd land somewhere between Dodák's orchard and Radko's pasture—only it's pitch black! We'd be rolling over rocks, thistles, cow

dung . . . and that huge, angry bull Radko keeps—I bet
he's down there, loose, in the pasture . . .

You're shaking your head—rocks, bulls, you don't care,
you just want to get home. But, Stefie, there is one other
thing . . . I didn't want to tell you, but I have to . . . Remember that town we passed through . . . pretty gardens, storks nesting on chimneys . . . There was that street
with the empty houses . . . the broken windows, boarded-
up doors, the signs in Hebrew letters— Stop shutting
your ears. Listen! The people who lived there hadn't
come back and—Stefie, look at me! There might not be
anyone waiting for us at home . . . Aunt Lena . . . hold me
tight, little one, you have to know this: Aunt Lena might
not be back . . .

Hey, you're shivering. Come closer, inside my coat.
And stop the whimpering. I mean no one might be home
yet, they could be coming from far away, and you know
how hard it is to get around . . . I think that's what worried Sergiu, that's why he didn't want us to get back to
our village tonight . . . Don't cry, little one, he is wrong.
Forget what I told you. Everyone's home, but we can't
get down there tonight. I don't see even that one light
anymore, I wouldn't know which way to roll. Let's slide
down this side of the hill, back to the village with the
lights. Sergiu would still be out, we can wash up, get into
bed before he misses us. I wish he were here now; he'd
wrap his army jacket around us, keep us warm, help us
get down. When he comes to the room tonight I'll ask
him to stop the pain in my ankle, he'll know how. In the

morning it'll be all better—we'll walk home together. I want Sergiu to be with us when we walk through our squeaky green gate.

You're hungry. The chocolate? One tiny bite? No, Stefie, I'm saving it, you know why. Your face is full of sausage stains from the times I secretly fed you at the Plčkos'—and tomorrow there'll be a few more smudges, brown ones, after you pull your head out of the mixing bowl. Be patient, you won't be staying hungry for long. I bet Sergiu saved us some supper. He always has a special treat for us, but tomorrow we'll have one for him: Aunt Lena's bread, the best in the world. On Wednesdays it comes out fresh from Tomáš's oven.

We'll start out early. When we get home, Aunt Lena will still be in her dressing gown, the same she wore the morning I left to stay with the Plčkos. She'll hear the gate squeak, she'll look out, then run down the steps. We will hug each other so long, so tight that my nose will itch from rubbing against her woolen gown the way it did then, almost two years ago.

The garden will just be waking up, smelling of wet earth and lilacs. Then before long the gate will squeak again—it will be Anka bringing home our loaf of bread . . .

REMEMBERING

Frost has painted beautiful white flowers on our window, and through their crystal leaves I can see the girls of our village carrying baskets to the house of Tomáš, the baker.

Noiselessly they tread up the hill in the chill morning air. Their small, upturned noses are red as the ribbons that perch on their braids like giant butterflies.

"Hey, Božena!"

Božena doesn't hear me. She is taking her shawl off her shoulders and winding it around the basket. The dough must be kept warm or there won't be any bread to eat!

Karla, with her little brother clinging to her skirts, has no scarf or shawl. Shivering, she hugs the basket and hurries to keep warm.

There struts Poluška, maid of the village doctor, in a fur coat—a hand-me-down from her mistress. The basket she carries is wrapped in a woolen blanket and covered with a lace-trimmed cloth.

I hear the familiar grating of the garden gate, and Anka, our maid, appears on the street. Cradling her bundle, she watches the girls and waits for one of her friends.

"Go on, Anka," I call to her. "Hurry!"

I can already smell the fresh bread we'll be eating for supper. My mouth waters at the thought of its crunchy, golden crust.

"Don't let the fire die," my aunt reminds Anka during supper. "It's Tuesday. We need to get the dough ready for the bread."

Logs crackle in the large kitchen stove while my enemy, the clock, ticks toward my bedtime hour.

"Aunt Lena, may I stay up and watch?"

She doesn't answer.

Does she know that the nut cake turned out shriveled because I kept tasting the batter while I mixed it? On Wednesday, when she called me to dry the dishes, did she see me hiding behind the woodshed? Is she still angry with me for smuggling out the hen that was to be our Sunday dinner?

My room is cold at night; it's far from the warm kitchen with its scent of cloves and green apples.

"Aunt Lena, may I please stay up?"

She ties a blue kerchief over her hair, rolls up the sleeves of her polka-dot blouse, then, smiling at me, nods. I settle in a cozy spot near the stove and wait for them to begin.

Anka remembers to weave her golden hair into a tight

braid. Hands scrubbed clean, she places the blue basin on a wooden stool. The basin is old, and where the enamel is chipped are dark spots of familiar shapes: a rooster's head, a sea horse, a witch in a pointed hat, a dragon, two monkeys with joined tails, and, last to appear, with a little help from my fingernail, the stern profile of Vojtech Rospačil, the principal of my school.

While Anka holds a sieve over the basin, Aunt Lena carefully tips the flour bag. Inside the basin a white mountain starts to grow. The peak rises toward the sieve, while tiny particles slide down the slope.

"That will do," says Aunt Lena when a white tip appears above the mesh. She hands the flour bag to Anka and in turn receives another. This time, a dark mountain rises alongside the white one. Of the two, the dark mountain is always the higher, unless we are celebrating a holiday or a birthday.

Anka keeps raising the sieve and the dark peak follows it. Aunt Lena turns around to sneeze. I look up, and in her place stands an old woman! She is wearing a white kerchief and from under it peek locks of white hair. Her eyebrows and eyelashes are white, a white mustache curves above her lip, one white hair sprouts from her chin. Anka winks at me—she, too, is white from the flour. She taps the wooden frame of the sieve, and leftover bits, too large to pass, bounce to the rhythm of her beat.

"Enough!" commands the strange old woman with the familiar voice. She empties a pot of boiled potatoes into the basin and crushes them with her fingers. The rough, uneven lumps spread out at the feet of the two mountains like a freshly plowed field.

"Water, please."

Aunt Lena bores wells in the fields while Anka aims the pitcher. Gurgling and bubbling, the wells overflow. Now there are ponds and lakes and thin streams groping for a path among the rough, uneven lumps.

"Don't forget the fertilizer!" I remind my aunt.

"The *what*?"

"Yeast," I explain. "And salt." And *frost*, I think to myself.

Anka's hand slips into the glass jar holding the caraway seeds. Her long fingers turn into tentacles of a monster reaching for its prey. The frightened seeds cowering at the bottom are cornered and seized. But now, fat with prey, the monster can't get out! Squirming and writhing, it tries to squeeze through the narrow opening of the jar, and as it does, some of its captives escape.

> "Birdies, birdies, fly away,
>   Promise to come back today,
>   If you'll keep away the rain
>   I will feed you golden grain,
>   *Unka-punka, hopla-hey,*
>   Birdies, birdies, fly awaaaaay . . ."

Reciting this in one breath, Anka swings up her arm and opens her palm. A cluster of birds rises to the ceiling, then swoops down and settles on the slopes and fields inside the blue basin.

With broad, circular sweeps, Aunt Lena's hand merges the landscape into a thick, yellow paste. It clings to her fingers and climbs up her arm toward the rolled sleeve of her polka-dot blouse.

Sweat trickles down Aunt Lena's temples and forms grooves in her flour-powdered cheeks. Her movements become more forceful, shorter and faster. Anka strains to hold down the basin as it bounces on the wobbly stool. The dark shapes of chipped enamel are now animated. The rooster's comb quivers, the sea horse spins, the two monkeys curtsy, the witch hat bobs, the dragon tosses its mane. And my school principal, Rospačil? I wish I could see him, but he is on the other side of the basin. I don't dare get up and move about.

Bubbles start to spout, making smacking sounds, like a baby. Aunt Lena can't stop to rest. She looks tense. I watch the polka dots on her blouse as they rise higher with each breath. Her hand moves so fast that I can no longer tell it apart from the swirling yellow mass that follows it. Anka's face is red. It looks as if she is going to let go of the basin and burst into tears!

Suddenly it happens: the dough, a smooth, bouncy lump, drops to the bottom of the basin. Aunt Lena sighs. Anka wipes her eyes on her sleeves and pinches my nose.

After such hard work we deserve a treat.

"Could we finish the nut cake, Aunt Lena? There is a small piece left."

My aunt does not look at me. She is looking at the dough. She is smiling at it, bending over and patting it.

"Aunt Lena, that cake will get stale!"

My aunt doesn't hear me. She sends me upstairs for a clean cloth. "The pretty one," she adds. "With embroidery."

"The one *I* am not allowed to use," I grumble.

She takes the cloth and covers the dough. She asks Anka to fetch the extra blanket from *my bed* and wraps it around the basin.

"I hope it will be warm enough," she whispers.

Anka and I also talk in whispers and move about on tiptoe, but still we're ordered out of the kitchen.

I hate that stupid dough!

The following morning Anka and I hold our breath as Aunt Lena uncovers the basin and lifts the cloth.

Did the dough rise? Will Aunt Lena be in a good mood or a foul one for the rest of the day?

Thank heaven, a good mood, the dough is almost spilling over the rim of the basin.

"Aunt Lena—"

"Ssssh." My aunt puts a finger to her lips. I mustn't talk. The sensitive creature in the basin might take fright.

Tenderly she places the dough on a board and pats it into an oval shape. She dips a feather in egg yolk to give it a shiny, golden coat. A white cloth sprinkled with flour lines the basket in which the dough is gently nestled. Aunt Lena's name, on a tag, is pressed into the underside of the dough and the corners of the white cloth folded over it.

"Go, Anka. If Tomáš burns this bread I'll burn his mustache. You can tell him that!"

Anka takes the basket and leaves the kitchen.

The house feels empty. It is still early; there is no rush to start the household chores. I watch Aunt Lena resting at the table, sipping a cup of coffee. A warm feeling inside me spreads and grows. I forgive her for having patted the dough and smiled at it, for having covered it with the embroidered cloth and the blanket taken from my bed. I walk over to my aunt and embrace her. She strokes my arm and kisses me on the nose.

"Saint Marta," I mumble, "please let Aunt Lena's dough turn into the most beautiful loaf of bread in the village!"

The front door opens. I rush to the window and through frost-painted flowers watch the girls as they trudge up the hill.

EPILOGUE

Katarína returned to her village. She found only
her teacher, Miss Sipková, to welcome her. The
teacher told Katarína that most of her classmates
and their parents were dead. They died in a fire set by
the Germans in retaliation for suspected partisan activi-
ties in the surrounding countryside.

Katarína waited in her teacher's home a year for her
aunt to return. She continued to wait even after learning
that Aunt Lena had died of typhoid fever in Auschwitz.

Only 11 percent of Europe's Jewish children alive in
1939 survived the war. The child who inspired *Katarína*,
long since grown to adulthood, lives in a small university
town in California. She writes stories and teaches music
to children, all the while holding on to her lost world in
memory.

About This Scholastic Signature Author

KATHRYN WINTER lives in Berkeley, California. Her short stories have appeared in various publications. In writing *Katarína*, her first novel, Ms. Winter has drawn on some of her own experiences as a Jewish child growing up in World War II Slovakia.